The Unofficial Not *ENTIRELY* True History of THINGS According to a Cat Named:

SAMMY JACK

a tall tail by
JINXI **BLUE**

TABLE OF CONSTANTS

.... Uh, wait...*Consonants*......, um, *continents?* Right....

THE LIST OF THINGS CONTAINED IN THIS BOOK FOR YOU TO READ OR MAYBE NOT IF YOU DON'T WANT TO.
Phew.

DEDICATION

To Pippin, my real life Sammy Jack:

You may not be able to speak in a way that everyone can understand, but we hear you just fine little girl. We hear you just fine indeed.

A very special thank you to Allan and his cats, for being the muse which inspired this story.

And to my grandparents…. you know why.

For all those animals who need to be loved as dearly as those who already are, a percentage of all profit gained from the publication of this novel shall be redirected to the many nonprofit organizations who dedicate themselves tirelessly to their wellbeing.

AN APOLOGY TO THE READER

I wish to sincerely apologize for the creation of this catastrophe.

It came about much of its own volition and I blame the presence of a keyboard, a silly imagination and a rather large amount of coffee consumption in its original conception.

I want you to understand that the rubbish which forms the foundation of this book is purely fictional.

It stems from a mind that spends far too much time thinking about round-a-bout things. Things like "How is it we came up with the words for colors?" or "Considering that the universe is infinite in every direction, how do we orient ourselves in the vast vacuum of space?"

And then there come even more deranged lines of questioning to follow up those other questions. In example: "Why is it we refer to space as empty, if there are all kinds of matter floating about in it?" and "If space is a vacuum, you would think it would be cleaner.

But then again maybe we are on the inside of the vacuum bag, which leads me to wonder what the outside looks like?

You see? I have done my part and warned you. That having been said, if you do decide to proceed, I hope you enjoy reading it as much as I enjoyed writing it.

Sincerely Yours;
Jinxi Blue

"The amount of happiness that you have depends on the amount of freedom you have in your heart"

~ *Thich Nhat Hanh* ~

CHAPTER ONE

A CAT WHO COULD SPEAK

Just because you think something is real doesn't make it real at all. Dawson Parks came to this anomalous conclusion – *for him anyway* - as he looked at his little ginger cat, Sammy Jack. He stared at her and she stared right back and in a rather nasty looking manner.

Of course, Dawson knew it was unfair to think Sammy was *deliberately* being nasty, after all, he had never thought to ask his cat why she always looked so cross.

So, on a rather spontaneous whim, he did just that.

Dawson folded his arms, furrowed his brow and asked: "Sammy Jack, why do you always look so bloody cross?"

Then he waited.

Dawson blinked and so did the cat. He blinked again and soon followed the cat. They blinked and stared until the full span of nine and one-quarter seconds passed.

It was then – *and very unexpectedly I might add* - something in the simple, straightforward, no-nonsense world of Dawson Parks, *happened.*

Now, before we go on, you must understand a few things about our unlikely protagonist.

You see, in Dawson Parks *regular* sort of reality, things that might be considered *unusual* or *unexpected* scarcely ever take place.

Dawson was an uninteresting sort of fellow; plain in personality, appearance, and action.

In fact, and let us be perfectly honest here, Dawson never did much of anything, other than the less notable of human activities.

Our friend enjoyed the regularity of routine. He was that kind of person who liked to eat the same thing each morning and dressed more or less the same each day, with only small and modest variations.

Average in height and average in stature, Dawson's brown hair was short cropped and always neatly combed, and he had eyes that were a nondescript hazel.

The man had no hobbies, no aspirations, no dreams and those few souls he might call his mates - *if he were more personable* - were just as outwardly uninteresting as he was.

To be fair to poor Dawson, he did - on occasion - have a bit of excitement in his life.

As a bank teller at the First Imperial Bank of Britain, or, F.I.B.B for short, he would sometimes be witness to a disgruntled customer causing a bit of a *stir*. Such situations were almost certainly unjustified of course, but nonetheless, scenes like those did tend to shake things up a bit.

Beyond that and the regular sort of happenings of life- indeed very regular in Dawson's case- you would not say that something unique or profound ever took place.

Nothing groundbreaking, nothing earth-shattering, nothing mind-blowing, no tomfoolery and certainly no hijinks.

Right, well, now that we have that sorted, we can move on to that thing which *DID* happen unexpectedly. Which would be the reason you bothered to read this far at all, wouldn't it? I mean, you must be very curious by now, considering how long you have had to wait.......

CHAPTER ONE

Sammy Jack - *the cat* - stretched and yawned and spoke back, much to Dawson's astonishment.

"Well, if you *must know*," The cat stated quite factually, "This is just the way I look."

She sat upright and waited for Dawson to process the situation.

After all, human beings are notoriously slow at absorbing new ideas. Especially ideas like that of a cat actually answering back, amongst other things.

In fact, for creatures that liked to brag about their evolutionary superiority and advanced minds, they certainly were against changes in what they perceived as *universal truth*.

"You....... *talked*......."

Dawson's brain suddenly felt as though it were a wobbly top spinning about in his skull. With a great deal of trouble, he tried to make sense of what he had clearly just witnessed- but it simply *could not be*. His cat could not possibly be answering him back. It was improbable, *nay IMPOSSIBLE* and yet...

"I spoke, yes." Sammy Jack's golden eyes narrowed and again she looked rather cross.

But then again, maybe Sammy was not cross at all. After all, she did just say that was simply how she looked. It could be that particular expression was meant to be mirthful and full of whimsy. Maybe it was a sardonic look or *maybe she really was cross*.

Or it could be she was simply agitated that he had asked why she always appeared cross, to begin with. After all, that manner of question could be considered rude in some circles.

Dawson just didn't know.

He felt his whole reality unraveling around him...... the universe was coming undone....... flying to pieces...

"Now stop that at once!" The cat's voice was firm and under noted with a spit and hiss.

Dawson froze, realizing he had, until that sharp reprimand, been pacing about his floor and whimpering like a child who had just experienced a frightful nightmare.

He pointed a shaky, accusing finger towards the errant feline.

3

"You……. you talked again……!" Dawson's own voice sounded very odd to him now - rather squeaky and uncertain.

The cat rolled her eyes. *Actually rolled her eyes.* What kind of cat rolls her eyes?

"I spoke again, yes Dawson. Shall we have another go on the merry-go-round? Or will you settle down and be reasonable?"

Dawson blinked, and stared dumbly at the animal.

It occurred to him that he was being rather unreasonable, and also very impolite. After all, it was he who initiated the conversation, to begin with. One can hardly blame someone for responding if you decided to ask them a question, even if they were a cat.

"Reasonable. Yes. Indeed." Dawson looked around himself as though he had lost something important. He patted his pockets, including that on his shirt, and tapped at his thighs.

There was no cause for the actions -as he had not lost anything at all- but he went through the motions anyway. *Nervous tension,* he blamed it on. It was not every day a man's cat starting talking to him in his living room, after all. He had every right to be frazzled.

Finally, he settled, plunking himself down into his old armchair without much ceremony. A relic from the past - like most of the furnishings in the apartment - the chair had clearly seen better days a long time before Dawson had ever rented the flat. Perhaps even a long time before Dawson was born.

It was a ratty, ancient looking thing; worn around the seams. It may have been a luscious and vibrant burgundy once. It might even have looked like an armchair fit for a king, or at least for nobility.

Now it was nearing the junk heap, with springs sticking out through its tattered upholstery and its color faded to a milky, pinkish hue; a color which was sickly looking at best. Yet, Dawson had a great fondness for the decaying thing, although he wasn't quite sure why.

With a resigned sigh, Dawson slouched into the chair and rubbed his temples. "I've finally snapped. I've lost my mind completely…."

Sammy Jack dropped down from her perch on the mantle of the apartment's de-commissioned fireplace and landed with an indelicate thud. She jaunted across the floor and then leaped onto the armrest of Dawson's shabby throne.

Sammy was a dainty looking cat, smaller than average and svelt. She had a little pink nose and plush, tabby print fur which ranged in color from dark pastel orange to cream. Her tail was fluffy and usually carried quite high. It had this endearing way of curling over just at the top - a trait which often made Dawson think of one of those feathered hats the three musketeers wore in the old films.

"Oh," She said in a tone that was clearly meant to be reassuring, "I wouldn't go as far as that, Dawson."

"You wouldn't would you?" Dawson gave the cat a sidelong look. "I'm talking with a cat. And the cat is answering back. There must be medications for this."

Indeed, all at once Dawson felt as though he had somehow stumbled down Alice's proverbial rabbit hole. He fully expected to find himself, at any moment, faced with the choice of whether or not to take a swig from a bottle innocently labeled *"Drink me"*.

"Why is it human beings are so opposed to the idea that animals can in fact talk?" Sammy Jack lay down with her legs tucked beneath her body as her tail drooped limply over the edge.

It was the way she usually sat in the window casement. There she would look outside for hours and watch the activity on the street below with a casual, passing interest.

"Well." And Dawson actually had to give it some considerable thought. "They normally *don't*."

If a cat could look exasperated, Sammy Jack certainly managed it in that moment. "Tsk. You don't normally speak Swahili either do you? But your comrades wouldn't lose their marbles if you suddenly learned a few choice lines in that language, now would they?"

"I guess not. Although to be honest, if I came out speaking Swahili all of a sudden, it might give them pause." Dawson sank deeper into the chair. "Where would I learn Swahili anyway? It's not as though one might simply sign up for a class at the local community center......."

Sammy Jack's golden eyes bore into him. It was a discomforting feeling.

He continued to ramble, casting his gaze about the room in an aimless fashion. "I suppose you would have to go to Africa...."

When Dawson managed to turn back to the cat, he began to feel incredibly overwhelmed.

It defied convention, a talking cat - or any kind of talking animal he supposed. Although he recalled that they had taught apes to use sign language. Apes were also fairly close to people in make and model, so it came as no great surprise they might be taught to communicate with their hands. Even so, they had not come straight out talking like Sammy Jack had and certainly not as fluently.

"Why are you talking?" Dawson groaned. "Isn't that physically impossible for cats? I mean, I am no biologist, but, do you not lack the appropriate physiological devices to convey words the way a human does? You sound an awful lot like my old gran, although she's been dead nearly ten years."

Dawson sank deeper still into the chair until the sensation of a coiled spring digging into his left buttocks deterred him from sinking further.

"Well, I am certainly not your grandmother's ghost, if that's what you are wondering." Sammy Jack's tail swished back and forth. "As far as biology is concerned, I am not sure exactly how I am able to speak human dialects, I just can. Most cats can understand human beings, but not all can annunciate your difficult and needlessly complex method of speech. I suppose that makes me special. Not that I consider it any kind of achievement."

The cat sighed deeply and kept a close watch on Dawson. "Look, you appear very pale. You aren't going to *vomit*, are you? I really can't stand the smell. I have a very sensitive constitution you see. So if you are going to eject the contents of your

6

stomach, please give me fair warning. At least have the courtesy of opening a window first."

Dawson hadn't considered that he was going to be sick, but something about the word *vomit* - especially the way she said it - struck him the wrong way and he found himself bolting towards the toilet.

He managed to topple over a floor lamp in the process and knock down several dusty picture frames from the wall on his way, but providence helped him reach the bowl on time.

You see, most times, the universe changes course very subtly. People hardly notice it at all. But there are very rare occasions when the universe comes full stop and turns right around in the middle of the highway of someone's life, causing more than just a little hiccup in the flow.

In fact, in some cases - like that of Dawson Parks - a traffic jam occurs; which was precisely why he ended up being sick. Some other people would have fainted - an option Dawson might have preferred. It would have tasted better.

"Are you alright Dawson?" Sammy Jack peered around the door frame.

Now seated upon the black and white tiles of the bathroom floor, Dawson moaned in the unhappiest of fashions.

Mustering as much energy as he could, he kicked out like an animated rag doll and slammed the door shut before the cat could enter.

He wanted nothing more to do with her until he was good and ready. And that would be a long while yet; this sort of situation was not at all his cup of tea.

It was Dawson's second revelation of the evening and it was not one he was enthusiastic about.

He had not had much experience with peculiar happenings in the past and had no interest in continuing along with this one either. After all, he was simply not the sort of person who this kind of thing should happen to.

According to the movies and many works of fiction, this sort of anomaly was supposed to happen to lonely children, or eccentrics or outcasts or other such characters.

It wasn't supposed to happen to Dawson Parks – but then again, that manner of thinking was the problem with folk like him.

You see, a person might think they know a thing very well.

They might know that what goes up must come down. They might know that every choice has a consequence. They might even know that the previous notion that what comes up must come down does not apply in the immense vacuum of space. That if one considered it very carefully, they might come to the conclusion that in space, there is no up or down.

And if one REALLY wished to complicate it further, one could surmise that as we, on this planet are floating about in space, there never really was any up or down here either. That depending on one's orientation upon the planet at any given time in its rotational cycle, we might be rather sideways, or upside down, or even backward.

When you look at things from that angle, you might start to question every notion ever claimed as being an undeniable truth.

That being said, there are many sensible people out there who seem to be enamored with a great deal of knowledge about the way that the world works. We shall refer to that well known and widely accepted array of ideas henceforth as *The Natural Order of Things*.

It is a concept entirely created by humans and it is regarded as infallible to humanity in general – until it becomes absolutely obvious that it is not. Periodically - and with great reluctance - one of the ideas is challenged. Usually, this is done by some avant-garde revolutionary who dared to look at things from a slightly different angle.

That is not to say that those same said rebels do not adhere to the other ideas contained within *The Natural Order of Things*. It only suggests that for a moment, a person decided that just because one has always accepted something as fact, does not mean that it is correct or the only way to look at it.

In general, this sort of person draws a great deal of negative attention towards themselves. After all, everyone knows that

8

their way of doing things differently or seeing things differently is absolutely absurd.

They are typically subject to being ridiculed and sneered at and are oft-times the butt end of very unfriendly jokes and snide observations.

The gossip crowd loves those sorts of people. Of course, eventually, it is realized that they might indeed be onto something. Then those same poo-poo -er's are the first to be singing their praises.

The whole scenario adds up to a great deal of foolishness, but then, that is the human condition; yet another well-established part of *The Natural Order of Things*.

Dawson Parks was not a radical thinker in any sense, and he was very much enamored with *The Natural Order of Things*. Indeed, he was a proponent of it. He quite enjoyed everything being just so and had no direct interest in changing that outlook either; although his cat seemed to have other ideas.

Because of this attachment to *The Natural Order of Things*, it would be a long while before Dawson could bring himself to leave the sanctified reality of the small tiled room he had exiled himself to.

It would be so long, that he would sleep in the tub that night; despite the unpleasant aroma of lemon scented cleaner and the lingering scent of sick and toothpaste in the air. His makeshift bed may have been physically uncomfortable, but at least his mind was put at ease.

Except for those occasional moments when the cat would inquire about his well-being.

When he didn't answer, she would mutter about how exasperating human beings could be, or about the smell of his being sick and her inability to open the window due to a lack of adequate phalanges.

A CAT WHO COULD SPEAK

CHAPTER TWO

PLAUSIBLE DENIABILITY

Morning came with a persistent ringing which bothered Dawson just enough to force him to come into semi-consciousness.

What was it anyways, carrying on the way it was?

He was not expecting guests, and it could not be his intercom anyways since he did not have one.

His mind felt so incredibly sluggish and hazy.......

Oh! The telephone!

Dawson erupted from his bathtub in an explosion of towels, and a scattering of bathtub commodities.

His movements were rather like that of a disjointed marionette operating under broken strings until he finally got his footing in the hallway. For a moment, he even forgot where the telephone was entirely and spun around in circles trying to locate the confounded thing.

Then the sounds of the unyielding communication device jogged his memory and Dawson raced for the black handset on the table behind him and answered.

"Hell... uh........?" His voice cut off in a sharp *unmphhh* as he simultaneously spoke and stubbed his toe on the sturdy oak leg of the console table on which the thing sat. His breath caught and he stifled the yelp that tried to assert itself from his throat.

Eyes wide, he proceeded to hop about on one foot, grabbing his throbbing toe in his hands and balancing the handset between his neck and ear.

If anyone had seen him just then, they might have thought he was doing a very bad impression of a lame kangaroo, or perhaps trying out a strange new form of Yoga.

After all, they had every other kind of Yoga; laughing yoga, sitting yoga, even yoga for dogs, or, *Doga*. Why not bouncing Yoga? Perhaps people would be more flexible if they hopped about while they stretched. They might even have more fun or less enticingly, more injuries depending on how they did it.

"Dawson? You all right?" It was his boss, Henry Wilkes.

Dawson fell over; he never was very good at the sock hop.

"Oh, yes yes. Sorry, Yes. Just fine. Yes." He stammered nervously as he picked himself up off the floor. "What can I do for you, Henry?"

"Well, sorry to bother you, but, I wanted to know when you planned on showing up for work this morning." Henry's voice was a bit anxious. Then again, Henry's voice was always a bit anxious.

He was the sort of fellow who always spoke with what sounded like reticence in his voice. It was as if he guarded some deep secret and was concerned about giving away too much information, even in idle conversation.

That was all well and good, but it made him sound ridiculous ordering coffee at the local café. How reserved does one need to sound when ordering a triple hazelnut latte with soymilk instead of cow's milk and whipped cream topping with a sprinkling of chocolate?

Then, it is rather odd to want soy milk instead of regular milk and then order whipped cream topping. One would suspect that to ask for soy milk in place of cow's milk would indicate a constitution unfavorable to the bovine boon. Then to order whipped cream - well - it just didn't fit. Perhaps Henry Wilkes was as shifty as his voice portended. Or perhaps he simply liked the flavor of soy milk. It was hard to say.

"Oh! Oh dear!" Dawson looked at the time on the wall clock. Half past ten, he was over an hour late!

Dawson's mouth went dry. *He was never late.*

In fact, in the ten years he had worked at the bank, he had never even taken a sick day.

He only took his holidays, which he was due, and he used them very practically to visit his few remaining relatives who were scattered about the country. Mainly, he visited his great aunt Charlotte. It was she who practically raised him while his mother went back to school and held a night job on the side after his father passed away.

"You've slept in haven't you Dawson? Guess you *ARE* human after all." Henry laughed. "Well, we were starting to wonder where you'd got to."

"I am so -*SO*- sorry Henry. I can explain. Well, I can sort of explain.......... Well, uh....... It was, um." Dawson stumbled over his words trying to fathom how he could possibly explain his evening without sounding like a raving lunatic. But then, did he actually know what happened? It all seemed to be a bit of a blur....

"Oh for the love of ......!" Henry huffed impatiently at his stuttering. "It's not the *end of the world* Dawson! Just get in when you can, you silly sod."

"Y-yes. Of course, Henry. Goodbye." With that, Dawson returned the handset to its cradle.

Clearing his throat, and running his hands through his hair, Dawson glanced around the quiet apartment nervously. Nothing seemed amiss. Everything looked just as it always did when he woke in the morning.

Except for the floor lamp that lay toppled near his feet, *that* wasn't where it belonged. He reached down and righted the thing grumbling incoherently to himself. Then there were a few picture frames which had fallen off the wall, so he straightened them out as well.

Already, he was trying to reconcile his mind to account for the unusual evening the night before, and his lack of responsibility that morning. He didn't drink, so intoxication was off the table.

Obviously.......... he must have fallen.

"I must have fallen in the tub........." Dawson murmured the words to himself as though saying them out loud would reinforce their validity. He walked back towards the washroom and gazed with displeasure at the disarray within. Towels were strewn, bathroom articles were toppled about. "Uh......What a *mess......*"

Still, considering the state of the room, Dawson felt more confident in his previous conclusion. With a long sigh, he felt a smirk tug at the corners of his mouth, but it never did quite make it all the way. He felt the wheels of reason and logic turning hard in his brain.

That is precisely what had happened, his mind asserted. He must have taken a fall in the tub and passed out from a concussion. A dreadful and dangerous accident for sure, but clearly, Dawson had survived the night.

What a relief!

Why he was in the tub fully dressed, Dawson did not know. What did it matter? Clearly, he must have been -*fixing*- something or other when the fall happened.

Yes, that must have been the way of it!

A very foolish and impulsive thing to do indeed. That is - of course - why it is better to have a professional come along and fix things. One does not have to suffer a concussion doing things one ought not to be doing if they leave it in the hands of a practiced tradesman.

Clearly, he would have to find out what the problem had been to begin with, to cause him to think he should fix it himself instead of phoning the repairman. It could not have been too complex. Dawson was not exactly the kind of man you would call handy, and had never taken an interest at all in learning to be.

Handiness was for fellows who wore trousers that didn't fit right and showed more crack then they covered. Dawson's trousers were not of that variety.

He had fallen and he had banged his head. It was a good, reasonable and solid explanation. The talkative cat had been a side effect. A very unusual dream brought on by his fall. As if to reassure himself of his distorted recollection, he reached back to feel if there was a bump on the back of his head.

He searched very hard. There must be something...

Yes, yes! There was a bit of what could have been a lump at the base of his skull. It must have gone down overnight. After all, he wasn't a physician, how was he to know how long a bump took to go away?

Comfortable with the excuse he had given himself, Dawson rushed about the small flat getting ready to go to work. Being late was an entirely new experience for Dawson and not a pleasant one either. It made him feel almost desperate to get out the door. He ended up tearing a perfectly decent dress shirt in his haste which served only to delay him further.

By the time he was ready to shave, he was feeling much better. Especially since he had figured out that he was not delusional and that he had taken a bad fall - not talked to a cat and had her answer back. A fall followed by a concussion was much better an explanation than an animal that suddenly decided to talk. It was much more reasonable - more realistic. More PROBABLE.

Now I ask: Have you ever noticed how when you think you have things all figured out, life throws a curve ball at you?

It's like a celestial game of chance, and it could be suggested that it is simply meant to keep us all on our toes. It was precisely that which happened next, and the timing could not have been more succinct to demolish Dawson's rationalizations.

"Feeling better Dawson?"

Dawson heard the voice from behind him just as he set his toothbrush back in its holder. It made his throat clench and his heart skip more than just a beat. In fact, it may well have started a game of hopscotch as he turned towards the sound, overcome with dread.

Sammy Jack strolled over to him, tail high in the air like a fluffy plume, and brushed against his leg in that way cats often did when they had an ulterior motive.

"Oh no! *No no no no no*......" Dawson shook his head miserably and shimmied past the small creature, nearly leaping out of the small bathroom to get away.

"Dawson please...." The cat spoke again but he cut her off.

"Now where's my watch? I could've sworn I saw it a minute ago........." He hurried about the apartment, searching for his watch and all the while muttering about the obvious residual effects of his fall.

"Dawson......" The cat said again, more firmly. "Dawson really...."

Why did she sound so sensible? He was falling to pieces, and she shouldn't even be talking. Clearly, it was just imagination – no - delusion, brought on by his accident. Surely it would pass, and she would go back to meowing and mewing like a regular, normal, non-talking cat.

"Not listening!" He yelled as he hummed a frantic tune that was meant to be something but ended up being nothing at all.

"Dawson, your watch is on the table." Sammy Jack's voice sounded exasperated.

"Ha! There it is on the table!" Dawson's eyes were wide with triumph as he held the watch aloft before slapping it on. "I knew I'd just seen it."

"That's what I just said, Dawson." The cat kept pace with his frenzied stride, minding not to get under his feet.

"Right, off to work!" Dawson grabbed his briefcase and slipped on his shoes.

"Before you go, Dawson......." The cat's voice was a bit more urgent.

"Nope! Can't talk, got to go. G-2-G, in text speak!"

"But Dawson I...."

16

CHAPTER TWO

He slipped out the door and shut it quickly behind him, cutting off the conversation and leaving the cat in the silence of the flat, twitching her tail in frustration.

PLAUSIBLE DENIABILITY

CHAPTER THREE

THE UNNATURAL ORDER OF THINGS

There are some very simple facts that most people know by the time they reach adulthood, and yet they disregard them entirely.

One, for example, is this: *Ignoring a problem does not make it go away.*

Alongside the conclusion that just because one thinks something is real, does not make it so, Dawson was now realizing that trying to ignore what had happened, was not making it go away.

It was less of a profound realization. In fact, you could hardly call it a proper realization at all since he had already been aware of it since his ascent into rational thinking. Instead, it was simply one of those stray thoughts that drift about at the back of one's mind but never sets anchor until something dreadful or avoidable happens due to your ignoring it.

So one might say that the notion of *Ignoring a problem does not make it go away*, is a universal truth. It was in this instance at least - even if Dawson was trying every mental strategy he could to prove that law wrong.

THE UNNATURAL ORDER OF THINGS

If one were to delve into the real issue at hand, though, one might find that the reason for his distress was that Dawson Parks was very accustomed to the *Natural Order of Things.*

What all of those things are does not need to be listed here - in fact, it is probable that you could already list quite a lot of them yourself. But among the myriad ideas on that list was the knowledge that cats did not talk - *not like a human being at any rate*- and they did not engage human beings in conversation either.

Cats purred when petted or meowed for food and did other such acceptable feline activities. Cats chased paper balls, played with catnip toys, and swatted and ate the occasional fly. Perhaps they also dreamed of things like catching birds and mice, or, if they were feral, hunted them on a regular basis. Cats do a great many things, and they do not do many others.

Talking was one of the many other things that cats were not supposed to do.

This internal struggle was waged throughout Dawson's workday. Was what he had experienced real or delusion? Had his mind become confounded somehow? Either way, the knowledge that he would have to go home at five o'clock and face up to the unwelcome disturbance to the *Natural Order of Things*, caused him a great deal of anxiety.

With mussed hair and last night's whiskers still on his chin, Dawson looked very unlike his usual self and it had not gone unnoticed by his co-workers. In fact, he had even forgotten to tie his tie and had to be reminded to do so by Doti Thomas.

Dorothy "Doti" Thomas was another bank teller at F.I.B.B. and a longtime colleague of Dawson's. She had come to work at the bank nearly eight years before and Dawson could still recall that day as though it had been yesterday.

She was a sweet-natured woman, kind and considerate towards others. Her hair was a sun kissed brown that she often secured in a tidy bun and she had rich brown eyes that were often hidden behind thickly rimmed glasses. Her voice bordered on a whisper and she did not speak often on a social basis.

CHAPTER THREE

Dawson was quite taken with her for the longest time, but could never work up the nerve to ask her for a date. So instead, he worked on being friends, which was the next best and safest thing to do.

In fact, it was Doti who had given Dawson the cat, as she couldn't keep animals in her flat due to regulations.

Apparently, she had found Sammy Jack wandering around the alleyway looking for a bite to eat, and so had started feeding her on the fire escape every evening around six o'clock. As time wore on, she realized that nobody seemed to own the cat, and when animal control came to impound the poor creature, she begged Dawson to please take the little kitty home. So he did.

That whole sequence of events had transpired a little over a month ago. Doti had been so emotional and convincing, and he had not seen any harm in it. The cat was no trouble, and she was very clean and well-mannered too. In fact, she seemed to be quite a regular kind of feline. Besides, having Sammy around meant all the more reason to talk to Doti and she even came around his flat a few times - to check up on the cat, of course.

Dawson helped another patron pay their bills and shift some funds around in their accounts. The morning had gone by a bit faster than he was accustomed to and the clock on the wall indicated it was approaching lunch hour.

Casting a discreet glance over in Doti's direction, he decided that it might be wise to inquire about Sammy with the one who found her to begin with. It only made sense; Doti had seen her first, so perhaps she knew something about it.

He and Doti ate lunch together just about every day across the road and a short jaunt down the street at a delightful café called *Yummies*. They both agreed that the name was quite accurate as everything on the menu there was, in fact, *yummy* and the owner, Richard, was on a first name basis with them now.

It would be a good place to ask Doti and avoid any unwanted eavesdropping at work. People were always so nosey at the bank. Dawson chalked it up to boredom - after all, it couldn't be called the most exciting place to find employment.

"What do you mean by that?" Doti smirked at Dawson's question as though she were waiting for the punchline.

Richard set out their food. "Anything else for you?"

"No. Thank you, Richard. This looks great." Doti smiled up at him.

"Thanks." Dawson took a drink from his freshened coffee cup and Richard wandered away to attend other customers.

The little place was full of people today, as was usual.

"What do you mean by *unusual tendencies*?" Doti chortled, repeating the last of what Dawson had asked her.

She really does have a lovely laugh; for a moment Dawson felt his mind wander back to the days when he was afflicted with romantic feelings towards his co-worker.

"Well," Dawson cleared his throat, focusing back on the issue at hand. "Well, you know. Did she ever do anything, or, maybe......... Perhaps make a sound that was not usual?"

Doti gave him a sidelong look. "Are you having fun with me, Dawson?"

"N-no! No, not at all." Dawson stirred up his vegetable soup, helping it cool a bit faster.

"Well, whatever do you mean then?" Doti's face suddenly grew quite grave. "Is she acting up? You know, now that she is settled in and all? Oh! I hope she's not one of those that tear the house apart."

"No, nothing like that Doti." Dawson smiled reassuringly. "She is very....... *vocal*, though. I just wanted to know if that was usual."

"Well, some are I suppose." Doti stated thoughtfully before she took a bite of her salad. She always ate such healthy foods, and she was a vegetarian. If she were more outspoken - Dawson thought - she might have been an advocate of animal rights. As things were, she supported causes by charitable donation and volunteer work.

"She really is no trouble." Dawson tried to reaffirm his commitment to the cat, although he was uncertain that the statement was, in fact, true. The cat had gone from being trouble-less to incredibly troublesome in the course of a single evening. "I've just never owned a cat before."

"Well, for one thing, Dawson," Doti's mouth turned up at the corners in a mischievous grin, "One never owns a cat, a cat owns you. I mean, you can own a dog or a horse. But not a cat, they have their own way of going about things."

Dawson smiled back, but he was bothered by that statement. "Like mind control?"

Doti leaned towards him looking quite serious now. "Yes. Exactly."

Looking quite disturbed, Dawson stared at his friend incredulously. Doti burst out laughing. "I'm *joking* Dawson. You're being quite odd today. Is something else bothering you?"

"No, well, I don't know." Dawson poked at his food. "I suppose I just didn't get a decent sleep last night.

"All right." Doti took another bite of her salad.

One of the qualities Doti Thomas had which Dawson appreciated was that she was not inclined to pry. Many people will poke and prod you for information, but not her. She believed it was better to allow people to talk in their own time, and on their own terms.

She would have made a terrible interrogator, but she made a lovely friend. Suspecting it was better to change the subject to something safer, like the weather or the news, Dawson turned to that instead.

Besides, in hindsight, he knew Doti would not want any more to do with as far-fetched a concept as a talking cat as he did. She was much too sensible.

There was also the matter of the fall he must have taken in the bath tub as well to consider and he did not wish to tell her that either, as then she would fuss.

Surely the cat would not be talking when he got home; after all, he was feeling much better now and he did seem to have all of his mental faculties intact.

THE UNNATURAL ORDER OF THINGS

CHAPTER FOUR

APARTMENT THREE-ZERO-ONE

Dawson didn't go directly home after work, although he did try to. When he stepped into the narrow entryway of the building, however, he found himself unwilling to ascend the staircase directly.

Instead, he decided to eat out and after that, he roamed the streets until it began to get dark. Only then, as the veil of sunset painted the sky in vibrant hues of purple and gold did he make an attempt to return to the little apartment on the third floor.

The tiny flat which Dawson had rented for the past seven years was much less in price or quality than he could afford, but he enjoyed being right around the corner from his job. Also - being a bit of a miser - Dawson enjoyed squirreling away the extra money into his bank account.

Nothing in the tiny apartment, save for the bed and his personal effects, was even his. The place had come furnished which suited Dawson just fine as well. It saved him the hassle of furnishing the place himself.

The day had been quite uneventful aside from the morning excitement. Nothing had seemed out of place.

Still, Dawson began to fret as closing time approached. Even Doti, who never pried, asked again if he was feeling well after lunch. He had simply answered that he was a bit under the weather. Given the terrible sleep he had the night before, that statement was not inaccurate.

Now, standing before the cracked green painted door of apartment three-o-one, the reckoning was at hand.

Summoning a great deal of resolve, he put his key into the lock and turned the latch. The door opened with a *squeeeeee* sound. The old hinges tended to do that, and Doti had told him several times to oil them.

Sammy Jack was laying in the hallway, staring at him and twitching her tail sharply in agitation. But, and he noted this with some relief, she said nothing.

"Hello, Sammy!" He said with his usual greeting and waited again, with knots in his stomach. Her tail swished and her ears laid back a bit, but still, nothing.

Dawson closed the door and took off his coat and boots. He arranged them respectively on the hanger and the shoe rack by the entryway. Sammy Jack still just lay there watching him quite intently.

With a deep sigh of relief, Dawson smiled to himself. "Right! Well, that's over and done with I suppose."

He started to walk towards the kitchen to put the kettle on when he was stopped dead in his tracks by a snippy retort.

"I'm hungry Dawson." Dawson turned slowly to look at the cat, who was now sitting.

"What?"

"I'm *hungry*. You didn't feed me last night, and you ran out this morning without feeding me either." The cat stood and took a few steps in his direction. "I'm quite famished, and lack the necessary functions to open my tin of food, so if you don't mind, perhaps you could do the honors?"

Dawson just stared. She was still talking. *Still. Talking.*

He was fairly sure that no other abnormalities had happened in his day. In fact, all in all, the day went by quite smoothly. He had seen other animals, well one anyways. An old miniature

26

schnauzer named Holly who frequented the bank with her elderly owner.

Holly hadn't spoken to him. Dawson had even said "How are you today Holly?" and Holly had done nothing more than loll her tongue out to one side and wag her tail in proper dog fashion. That compliance to the way things ought to work had earned her a biscuit.

"Dawson! Really! *I'm starving!*" Sammy Jack pleaded miserably breaking him from his stupor.

"Right." Dawson wandered into the kitchen and opened the cupboard door. There were several different tins of Posh Kitty dinners and somehow he couldn't decide which to give her. "Ah, which sort did you want?"

Sammy Jack jaunted into the kitchen, tail high in the air. "Is the seafood one there? That *Mariners Delight* one is my favorite. Dear me, I'm so hungry I believe I could eat a whole tin!"

Dawson grabbed out the tin labeled *Mariners Delight: Three Fish Blend.* On the label, there was an exuberant looking cat and some gleeful looking fish. Why the fish would be delighted about being eaten by a cat, was beyond him. Marketing departments could be very morbid at times.

Without much ceremony, he pulled back the cover on the tin, plunked the smelly contents onto Sammy's plate and set it down on the kitchen floor. He watched her a moment as she began to devour her food, before exiting to go plunk himself down in his ratty armchair.

"I don't think tea's going to cover tonight, no…." Dawson massaged his temples. "No, perhaps a good stiff drink."

From the kitchen, Dawson could hear the dish clanging a bit on the tiles. A pang of guilt turned his stomach. Sammy Jack was never that ravenous, and he felt very bad over having neglected her.

Although he had never grown up with animals, Dawson prided himself on being a very diligent pet owner. If a person was going to have an animal, he figured that the animal's needs should all be properly addressed. After all, they were a bit helpless to control their circumstances. Sadly, not every pet owner thought the way he did.

"Delicious Dawson, *really!*" Sammy Jack called from the kitchen, clearly between mouthfuls. "Although I do find it a bit more appealing when you mash it up with the fork."

"*A talking cat.......*" Dawson sighed. "Why a cat?"

Sammy Jack emerged from the kitchen licking her chops. "Well, because *we are cats*, Dawson. We know just about everything."

Dawson raised a brow watching her pace towards him across the floor. "Now that's just rubbish. Nobody knows everything."

"Cats do." Sammy Jack jumped onto the arm of the chair and met him eye to eye. "Just about anyways. We are born knowing mostly everything...... it just takes us a bit to remember what it all is."

"And how long is that exactly?" Dawson raised his brow.

Sammy looked quite thoughtful for a moment before replying. "About a year and two-thirds."

"A year and two thirds?" Dawson's tone was skeptical.

"Yes, a year and two-thirds." The cat gave a quick nod and then proceeded to lick her paw and brush it over her head before stopping to add something as a side thought.

"That is, of course, a ballpark figure, so to speak. For some cats, it might be a year and three-quarters. The *slower* ones anyways. They don't tend to remember as much. Some of us, nowadays, hardly remember a thing."

"This all seems a bit silly." Dawson groaned and slouched back in the chair. "Talking to a cat, who claims to know everything because she was born knowing everything? Ludicrous."

"Well, I did have to remember it all...." Sammy chimed in.

"Over a year and three-quarters, yes." Dawson rubbed his eyes.

"A year and two-thirds actually. I am not one of those slow cats." Sammy finished grooming her face and lay down on the arm of the chair, tucking her paws beneath her in her usual way. "Also, I only know *mostly* everything."

"Right."

Sammy Jack sighed. "Look, the whole reason I decided to talk with you, is this: I need you to do something for me, Dawson."

"What would that be, pray tell?" Dawson muttered without enthusiasm.

"Well, I would like you to write a book on my behalf. You see, as with being unable to open a can of food, I am also unable to write and publish a book." Sammy Jack looked at him expectantly.

"I don't know about that." Dawson shifted uncomfortably. "It's not that simple. Besides, I don't even have a typewriter."

"Tsk. Nobody uses a *typewriter* these days Dawson. They use computers." Sammy blinked.

"I don't have a computer." Dawson had never seen any point in owning a computer. On the few occasions he did feel the need to look something up or send an email; he did so from work or the library. He did know how to use one, very well in fact, but why buy something that you can use freely?

Sammy Jack rolled her eyes at him again. "It's not as though you don't have enough money to buy one. Besides, you can take it all down in notes at first."

"I suppose I could get a laptop," Dawson stated hesitantly. "I've seen some that are affordable."

"Sure! It will be fun Dawson, and after the task is done, if it suits you, I will never say another word. I will go back to being just a regular, ordinary cat. To your standards anyways."

Dawson regarded the feline suspiciously. "What sort of book is this?"

Sammy Jack shifted a bit enthusiastically. "The Official History of Things: As Told by a Cat"

"Sounds like it will be a rather long book." Dawson said thoughtfully.

"Not really. There's not much to tell, honestly." Sammy made a motion that may have been a shrug on a human being, but on a cat, looked strange. "I just feel I need to set the record straight, after letting humans have their way with it for so long."

Now in the life of every person comes a moment where they must make a decision so pivotal that their very future will depend on the action they take just then.

Dawson was not entirely aware of the magnanimous choice he had to make in that moment, nor how it would affect his life, both present, and future. Perhaps if he had known, he would have thought a bit harder about it.

Then again, perhaps the reason we are so often unaware of the importance of these decisions is so that we do not give pause and instead act on instinct. Truth be told, Dawson didn't consider anything much on the subject, beyond Sammy Jack's promise to go back to being a regular cat.

After all, who was going to read a book like that? And besides, how hard could it be?

"Sure, why not. We can start tomorrow, it's the weekend, and so I don't have to work." Dawson took a deep breath, feeling a weight lifting off his shoulders. Things would soon return to normal.

"Oh! Splendid Dawson, really!" The cat's golden eyes closed and she began to purr loudly. "It should only take the weekend. Well, maybe more than that but lovely! I really owe you, Dawson! What a fine fellow you have turned out to be."

"Well. We'll see about that. I never was much good at writing."

Dawson rose from his seat and returned to the kitchen to start the kettle. He wasn't entirely sure as to what he was getting into, but best to get it over with as soon as possible.

CHAPTER FIVE

EVERYTHING YOU KNOW

"There is a fundamental rule you must follow Dawson if this is going to work."

Sammy Jack watched intently as Dawson settled into the armchair and opened up his notepad. It was a lovely spring day outside. The birds were chirping in the trees and a cool breeze came through the open window, bringing freshness to the apartment it hadn't known since last fall.

The breeze was uplifting, carrying with it the subtle hint of flora and the occasional, delicious waft of fresh bread and rolls from the bakery just across the street.

"What rule?" Dawson scribbled a few chaotic lines onto the corner of the first page to make sure the ink of the pen was flowing.

"You must accept that everything you know, everything you have ever known and everything you will ever know should always remain in question." Sammy Jack settled on the armrest and her golden eyes were focused on Dawson.

"Surely not everything?" Dawson questioned with a snort.

"Everything," Sammy said with finality. "You see the truth is the truth, but it is always reinterpreted in the eyes of the

beholder. Ergo what most people claim as irrefutable truth is in fact, irrefutable perception. And when truth becomes perception, Dawson, we must deal with the perception, not the truth."

Dawson gave it some thought. And then gave that thought some more thought. He had never looked into the things he accepted as real or true with any kind of critical process. If a scientist in a lab said it's true, then it must be. If an archaeologist said it's true, then that must be how it all happened.

After all, who was a bank teller to question the workings of history or the world at large?

"Another thing is that the universe is in a perpetual state of change. Not always in big ways, but mostly in small ways that add up to big things later on." Sammy Jack turned to watch a bird flutter by the window.

Dawson had to give that some thought too. He had always considered the universe a rather solid thing. That it all worked in a certain way, and that human beings were simply uncovering the way it worked as we went about the business of acquiring knowledge.

However, if what Sammy Jack claimed was true, then a great deal of effort was being put into trying to pin down a truth about something that had no truths at all. In fact, in that sort of scenario, labeling anything as fact in present tense was an enormous waste of time.

"All right, Dawson?" Sammy Jack cocked her head to one side, waiting for his answer.

"Right. Cheers." Dawson wrote that bit down. After all, it seemed a thing worth remembering on paper.

"So," Dawson puzzled, finally accepting that there was potential behind what Sammy Jack claimed. After all, up until a few days ago, he would never have believed in a million years that a cat might talk, at least not in a way he could understand. Given that everything we know should always remain in question, Dawson decided the best course of action was simply to take Sammy Jack's word as it was and leave it at that.

"So you know everything? You were born knowing everything?" Dawson stumbled over his words as he put pen to paper in his notepad. He felt like he was playing the role of a journalist in a stage play which had no script. It was unfamiliar waters for him.

"Well, everything that would matter to a cat, or, more accurately, everything a cat might choose to remember. That is of course why the book is entitled *The History of Things as Told by a Cat*, not *The History of Everything*." Sammy Jack lifted a paw to her mouth and licked it before sliding it over her head, then repeated the motion.

Dawson had to wonder, in that moment, why it was that cats seemed to do two functions primarily; groom and sleep. It was a distracting thought and it pulled him away from his task for the span of the average hiccup. It wasn't as though they were legitimately dirty in appearance when they decided that they should groom themselves, they just did it.

If anything and Dawson knew this was a stretched bit of reasoning, it would come across that both grooming and sleeping were not even conscious decisions on behalf of cats, but instead, unconscious; as much as blinking or breathing was.

"Well, where would you like to begin, Sammy?" Dawson shook off the idleness of his mind and came back around to what was trying to be accomplished.

"At the beginning would be best, I suppose." Sammy Jack stretched and yawned, arching her back before settling into her seat again.

"At the beginning?" Dawson puzzled. "Like the beginning of cats?"

"More like the creation of the universe." Both cat and man held each other's eyes for a few beats.

It took Dawson a few more to process what the cat was implying. After all, human beings had tried at great extent to find the answer to the age-old question of *"How did it all come into being?"* Here the answer was being offered quite freely and matter-of-factly to a fellow who had never had much interest in the subject at all by none other than a *cat* that seemed confident she knew what she was talking about.

The whole idea was preposterous.

"The creation of the universe?" Dawson scoffed. "You have the answer to that?"

"Sure." Sammy Jack didn't waiver under Dawson's skeptical retort. The whole scene took on the feeling of a high-stakes poker game. Yet it could hardly be said that there was any reason for it to be so. Unless you considered humankind's tendency towards cynicism. Then the stakes might be very high indeed.

"Right. So, what happened then?" Setting the notepad and pen down on his lap, Dawson crossed his arms and waited for what she had to say.

"Well," The cat began thoughtfully and then paused. She looked as though she were puzzled, "How to explain this in a way you can understand....... You see, there was another universe once."

"Another universe?" Dawson piped in.

"Yes." The cat sighed. "Several of them actually, if truth be told. Although I don't know much about those other ones. Anyhow, the *beforehand* universe was quite different than this one, yet quite a lot the same."

"One day," She continued, "I believe it was the equivalent of a Thursday, a sentient being - that was not at all like a human being - thought of a concept so profound, so obscure, that the laws of universal physics and the laws of universal normality collided and then whole thing unraveled and collapsed in onto itself."

"Then, after quite some time, the laws re-arranged themselves, and when things smoothed out, the universe came back into being, and things started to happen again."

"So, like the Big Bang?" Dawson pondered.

The cat carried on. "Well, not really. But, since trying to make you understand something as multidimensional as the thought process of an entity as enormous as an entire universe would probably make you go insane, we shall say that the *Big Bang* was close enough to count, yet still miles away from being on target."

"Miles away from target? I don't understand." Dawson shifted uncomfortably, trying to wrap his mind around what the cat just said.

It probably wasn't a very good idea to try to wrap his mind around an idea like that. The problem was - as it was with most people - rationalizing things was a knee jerk reaction. Kind of like seeing something you find incredibly distasteful and not being able to look away.

Sammy Jack shook her head. "Things are not always simple, Dawson. At least, not to explain in words. You see, the universe is not three dimensional. We just happen to exist in three dimensions."

"That doesn't mean that all that exists is three dimensional, it just means that all you can comprehend is in three parts. If you have ever noticed, three plays a rather large role in human concepts. Every so often, there is more, but you can always break it down to three if you look at it. It is because you are limited to three dimensions. It's sad, really."

Dawson played around with the idea in his mind. He turned it, tilted it, pushed it right side up and inside out and over and under and every other manner of way of looking at it before he came to the conclusion that he just wasn't sure how to feel about it.

"We do have squares. We have rectangles and even octagons, hexagons, tetrahedrons and all sorts of other things. We even have spheres and they have no sides at all. Well, they do have one I suppose, that stretches out over everything."

Sammy Jack just sort of looked at him and blinked, as though he was some sort of unfortunate thing that deserved pity. It was a discomforting expression, to receive from a cat.

"I would attempt to explain the depth of scope behind the way it all breaks down to three, but I believe we would be at it for much too long. My biggest fear is that in so doing, you might get wise to a notion that will reset the whole universe again. I really don't want to put the laws out in that way, it took them quite a long time to get sorted out the last time. And of course, add to that life would have to start all over again...."

Feeling a bit defeated, Dawson picked up the pen and notepad again and started writing in messy point form what they had spoken of.

As he scrawled the abbreviated conversation onto the unlined paper, he got that feeling you get when someone is looking over your shoulder. In this case, the feeling was very accurate, as Sammy Jack had, without his knowledge, shifted positions.

He turned his head slowly towards her offending presence as she leaned over his shoulder, looking at what he was writing as he wrote it.

Of course, when she realized he had stopped writing entirely and was giving her instead a very disapproving look, she cleared her throat and went back to her position on the armchair leaving him to finish in peace.

"Sorry Dawson, just making sure you have it all down right." She tried her best to mimic a human smile, but it instead appeared more like a fanged threat.

Dawson startled when he looked up from the paper to see her do that and dropped the notepad and pen in the process. "Good lord!"

"What?" Sammy Jack stood quite abruptly at his reaction, her tail twitching.

"What was that?!" Dawson exclaimed, looking at her with utter mortification.

"I was trying my hand at smiling. You humans seem to have the knack for it." Sammy sat back down and tilted her head to the side as Dawson retrieved his writing implements.

"Well. Don't do.... *that.*" Dawson settled back in to finish his writing with a scowl on his face.

"What's wrong with the way I smile? Am I doing it wrong? I daresay, I suppose cats lack the appropriate muscles to smile correctly."

Dawson sent her a sidelong look. "It looks.......... *disturbing.* Like something from a horror film. Sorry, but it honestly does."

"Oh." Sammy Jack shifted uncomfortably. It is never nice to have somebody tell you that you have a dreadful smile, and that sort of displeasure was not lost on a cat either. Dawson finished writing.

Seeing her dejected appearance, Dawson sighed. "Look, cats always seem to have a smile on their face, it's the way your mouths turn up at the corners. You don't need to show teeth. It makes you look fierce is all."

"I see." Sammy started to groom again. "So what have we got so far?"

"In a nutshell: That there were many universes that pre-date the one we are in."

"That when a sentient creature decides to go thinking about things that they ought not to think of, there is a slight risk of universal implosion and that even though humans do have a multi-faceted understanding of all manner of things, we are in truth limited to three dimensions."

"Therefore, we can only truly understand things as they relate to threes."

Dawson took a deep breath and looked at the cat who was giving his synopsis a good deal of thought. It occurred to him then that all she had in fact given him was a synopsis herself.

Finally, Sammy Jack stood and arched in a big stretch. "Right! That's good for now. Time for a nap!"

She hopped off the chair and started to walk in the direction of the bedroom, leaving Dawson a bit bewildered.

"What, that's it for now? We just barely got started!" Dawson stood, holding the pen and notepad limply at his sides.

"I'm tired. You do know that cats sleep a great deal right? Two-thirds of our lives, in fact, are spent sleeping." Sammy Jack yawned.

"Well, that seems an awful waste." Dawson grumbled.

"It might be." The cat resumed her journey to the bedroom. "But then again humans waste rather a lot of time being awake if you really look at it."

With that, the cat was gone.

No doubt she would soon be curled up on the foot of his bed where she enjoyed sleeping the most. Especially when the curtain was drawn and the sunlight hit the bed just so, like it would be today.

Dawson decided to add that last bit into his notes; about the slumbering cats seemed to deem a necessary use of their lives. It may be that it was through their dreams that cats remembered everything they were supposed to remember.

And if they did indeed have to recall the memories of an entire universe, and if it took a great deal of sleep to do so, it made sense that they spend most of their time inert.

So then one might say that a cat's version of sleep is like the quiet moment one takes to reminisce about old times. Dawson wrote that bit down as well.

CHAPTER SIX

THE GREAT TELLING

Ideas can be a rather like a seed. At first, they may seem very small, or otherwise unremarkable. They may not look like they could become anything much at all. But as anyone who has ever kept a garden might say, given time, a little sunshine and a few drops of rain and what happens next might just surprise you.

Dawson had never considered the precarious state of affairs life and the universe were in before his conversation only a short half hour ago with his cat. That life could be wiped out throughout the whole world; indeed, that the entire universe itself would come undone because of a singular realization that ought not to have been made was an unnerving prospect.

Despite being fully conscious herself of the direness of the revelation she had given Dawson - *just off the cuff* - as though it should be common knowledge, Sammy seemed unaffected by it.

It did not make any sense.

In fact, it really did not seem to bother the cat at all that life might just end without warning.

As he crossed the road, the very idea of the impermanence of it all started to eat away at him. It lingered and poked and pried and pulled at his consciousness. With every step, he tried to distance himself away from it and the tiny apartment on the third floor.

Sammy Jack had still been napping without a care when the scents and smells wafting through the window from the bakery finally drew him out. A lot of people were out on the street that day, none of whom Dawson knew, or would ever know.

People whose lives should be able to continue, un-ended by something as inane as a rogue thought. People, he realized, who were just like him.

Well, perhaps not just like him, some were really quite interesting, whereas Dawson was not very interesting at all.

Some were more callous, some were crooked, but most he thought, must be decent sort of folk.

They all made up the myriad faces of the unknown masses, except amongst their inner circles. It was then that Dawson - who was quite distracted by the end of the universe - ran into a fellow who was less distracted and in more of a hurry.

They collided quite haphazardly, and without grace in the middle of the crosswalk.

"Corr! Watch where you're goin' mate!" The man scoffed with a great deal of agitation, shoving past Dawson quite irritably.

"S-sorry." Dawson made an awkward job of apologizing before bounding to the curb, as traffic was even less patient than the fellow he had collided with and many horns started to flare up.

Dawson stared at the man, who gave him a glaring look backward as he walked away on the opposite side of the street, as well as a rude gesture which caused a few other looks Dawson's way. It occurred to him that the man had a point.

Not so much about the obvious need to watch where one is heading when they walk any place, but more, the less obvious side of it.

Turning left, he headed towards the bakery. His thoughts were even more troubled. *How many of us really watch where we are going?*

At the bakery, he ordered a coffee instead of tea, which was quite odd for him, accompanied by a few spiced cookies. Then he took a seat outside on the patio and watched the other folk walking by.

On the street that morning there were mothers with children, lovers, sisters, brothers, aunts and uncles, even perhaps a great granny or two.

There were youths and seniors, business people, scamps, the downtrodden and the upper class.

But how many, he thought, really paid attention? He knew all at once that he didn't. A great many people thought they paid attention. They made plans, and some even followed through. They looked towards the future with goals and dreams in mind. They worked hard. They kept a stiff upper lip and they kept their nose to the grindstone, all so they could be comfortable – *hopefully* - at some point. So they could achieve whatever it was they were shooting for.

But say they were all in full knowledge that through an act of complete randomness – *something as intangible and mediocre as a passing thought* – everything could be snuffed out.

All of their dreams, their hopes, their goals, their beliefs, were just gone - as if they had never really meant anything at all. And no trace would remain that they had ever existed at all.

It was a crushing thought to Dawson. A thought that was as physically painful as a hard slap. He realized as well that he was just as guilty as anyone of relying on a future that may or may not exist.

It all seemed well enough. Life was fairly normal on the streets of the city early on a Saturday morning. There were people laughing and talking on cell phones or laughing and talking with each other, or even doing a bit of both. One fellow walked past in a suit who looked none too happy as he did anything but smile or laugh into his cell phone. One poor young lady walked straight into a lamp post whilst texting and her friends erupted in laughter as they started to text what had happened to everyone they knew on their cell phones.

In fact, everyone seemed quite attached to their cell phones these days and Dawson didn't even bother to own one.

Perhaps all the better, he thought as the girl was aided to her feet by her cackling entourage.

Dawson could not quite figure out why he was so affected by the cat's revelation. He couldn't say for sure whether it was accurate or not. But as he had decided to accept that the cat could in fact talk, he, in turn, had to accept the fact that everything he knew should remain in question.

After the span of an hour went by, and a great deal of mulling over and over on the subject of how impractical the universe was to allow itself to be so easily usurped, Dawson headed home.

As he let himself back into the apartment, Sammy Jack strolled out of the bedroom and stretched.

"Did you bring me anything?" The cat spoke through a heavy yawn.

Dawson shook his head as he hung up his jacket and slipped off his loafers.

"Figures. You never do." Sammy headed back to the arm of the chair and settled there where Dawson soon joined her and slumped down into it looking quite dejected.

The cat tilted her head to the side and blinked at him through her golden eyes, which were half closed in the light cascading through the open window.

"Whatever is the matter, Dawson? You look quite morose."

"How can I not be?" Dawson muttered. "Given what you told me earlier."

"Did I say something terrible? I don't seem to recall doing that…." Sammy Jack looked as though she might seriously be pondering the idea.

Dawson glared at her. "Sammy! You told me that the last universe ended because of a simple thought."

The cat's eyes widened a bit. "Well, I wouldn't say it was a simple one. Actually, it was quite complex and took the creature involved over three hundred years to come up with. I daresay she was quite driven, although I cannot for the life of me remember what it was she sorted out."

"Are you saying you were there when it happened?" Dawson looked at the cat incredulously.

"Of course. Or else how else would I have remembered it? Sometimes I wonder at your skills of deduction." Sammy licked her paw and brushed it over her head. "I must say, you've taken quite a mood swing. I don't know what your problem is. You should be happy I told you. No human has ever known the real truth of it before, at least, not that I know of."

"Sammy Jack! You've told me the whole of life is essentially without meaning." Dawson groaned and sank into the chair even deeper, as though trying to dissolve into it completely.

"When did I tell you that? Life is full of meaning. Whatever gave you that idea? Really, Dawson, you are so negative about things."

"What's the point of it then Sammy? If life can be snuffed out as easily as that." Dawson groaned again.

Sammy Jack stepped down into Dawson's lap and curled up. Without thinking, Dawson reached down and began to run his hand over the soft warmth of her fur. It was an action he had become accustomed to doing since he had brought her home. There is something very soothing about petting a cat. It calms the nerves and steady's the beat of one's heart by lowering the blood pressure.

"It is not news that should be so overwhelmingly foreign to you Dawson," Sammy stated softly, and with some kindness. "Life on this planet could end just as abruptly and without warning due to any number of causes.

A rogue asteroid could strike the earth, or an exploding star, or a celestial event. These things are outside the realm of yours, mine or anyone else's control and are in fact far more likely than a universal collapse. The last universe was three times older than this one when it happened you know."

"Is that supposed to make me feel better?" Dawson muttered, taking his hand away.

"No." Sammy Jack continued. "But it should perhaps give you pause to appreciate how precious life really is."

Dawson's cheeks burned hot and a single tear rolled down the left side. "It's like; all we do is live then die, right? If what you have said is accurate, our lives are essentially....... *meaningless*, even *gratuitous*. So what would be the point Sammy, of all of it?"

"There is more meaning Dawson than you could ever conceive in this single lifetime or the next. It is more than the human mind can grasp at this stage, although you can catch a glimpse of it."

Sammy Jack's eyes sort of glazed over, as though she were looking somewhere very far away. "All of it, every second, every chance, every choice. Oh, my dear friend, I only wish I could show you the tapestry. Science will bring you only so far; the rest lay in an entirely different kind of understanding. It is a *portrait* Dawson, and the universe is the artist.

Call it divine, call it *God*, call it whatever you must, but understand that there never is, never was and never will be a proper word to express that which encompasses it entirely.

All around you Dawson! It is all around you! In every planet and every star and every galaxy! Oh, how I wish you could see it! How it stretches out through space and time, and to witness how *no part of it is ever truly alone*............

How you, and I and the little mouse in the hall and the fly on the wall, are all a part of the artistry of it.

How small we are in the greater picture, and yet, no less precious than any other part of it."

"But what's the point, Sammy? What's the meaning?" Dawson's chest felt heavy, sorrowful. He felt as though he were standing on the precipice of some high and lonely place, and that any moment he might fall into oblivion.

"To feel love. To be enthralled, entranced, delighted. To grieve, to lose, to be torn asunder only to have to rebuild ourselves from the wreckage." Sammy put her paws on his chest and was nose to nose with him now. "To EXIST."

Dawson's eyes snapped up to Sammy's.

44

The walls collapsed, the barriers, the preconceived notions ran out of him in a torrent, and it was just Dawson, and just Sammy Jack, and just the universe and all that it offered. For the first time in his life, Dawson felt free. Free to just be he. Free as we all wish we could feel, unbound, undone.

He let the tower crumble; he let his world tear itself apart. He would rebuild something better, something other than all he had reconciled himself to.

"We are a part of a grand story Dawson." Sammy lowered herself to be seated once more on his lap. "A great telling which is very long and very wide and which is made up of many smaller bits and pieces. Some stories are very small indeed. Some stories only have a short few moments then die. But all of them make up the tapestry. All of them are noted and important. We all write our own parts, and so it has always been. It is always we who decide which part we wish to play. So you asked me for meaning? There it is; *free will*. Choice.

How will you choose to have your story written Dawson? What memory will you leave behind?"

Dawson stroked her back very softly and wept.

"It's okay Dawson." Sammy purred loudly. "It's okay."

THE GREAT TELLING

CHAPTER SEVEN

MEANINGFUL ACCIDENTS

Morning changed into afternoon and Dawson was once again jotting down points and statements about the dialogue between him and Sammy Jack.

Dawson was feeling much more focused and indeed better about all things in general by this point. Even so, he was still overcoming the hurdles of his own deeper mental programming.

"What you should really be taking away from all of this Dawson, is that most major leaps in evolution or ideas occur accidently." Sammy sounded frustrated as Dawson tried to wrap his head around her last short dialogue about how life evolves into being advanced technologically.

It was actually quite a simple thing as far as the cat was concerned, but Dawson, being human, had to poke at it.

He stared incredulously at the cat. "Well, I don't agree that is entirely true. Some must happen due to creature's sort of, *working it out*. I mean, look at my species, and the creation of fire..."

Sammy Jack blinked as she observed him in that way which stated she was about to point out how extraordinarily foolish he was. Then, instead, she burst out into uninhibited laughter - laughter that was very odd, but certainly discernable as laughter, given that she was also able to talk.

To anyone else, it would have sounded more like a spastic fit of spitting and hissing, as though she had a hairball lodged in her throat.

Dawson crossed his arms and scowled. After all, he didn't see what was so funny. Everyone knew humans were the ones who developed the skills to produce fire.

"I really don't see the humor in that."

Sammy Jack continued laughing, trying to stifle it at great length, but without success.

So Dawson decided to continue. "Well, it's not as though cats could produce fire at will. It's not as though cats invented anything. Your kind rather just lies around and lets everyone else do the work. At least my kind was clever, and tried to make life better for themselves."

"Right. *Better.*" The cat finally managed to calm herself.

"I certainly don't hear any complaints from your end when I open up your ready-made food." Dawson was feeling quite peevish because of her outburst.

"No, no. You are right Dawson; it's just how it came about that I find so funny. And trust me; it wasn't through any kind of genius." Sammy Jack chuckled again before suppressing herself.

"How then?"

She cleared her throat. "Well, for that, you have to go back a very long time. So long ago in the history of your species, that, they were hardly your species at all yet."

"What, when we were *Neanderthals?*" Dawson had set aside his journal and pen. He folded his arms across his chest.

Sammy sat up and looked very thoughtful. "Further back than that and besides, those poor Neanderthals had nothing much to do with your people, except in passing."

"I thought we were descended from Neanderthals." Dawson cocked his head to the side.

Sammy slowly shook her head. "No Dawson, you aren't. Humans have managed to work that out already on their own. There was a bit of mixing, but, those gentle creatures developed apart from you."

"What happened to them?" Dawson tilted his head quizzically.

Sammy Jack's tone hinted towards sadness for a breath. "That can come after."

"Alright......"

"You wanted to know about fire, correct?" The cat's voice perked up as though she were sitting on the most enormous joke ever conceived.

"I don't know now. You seem to think it quite funny."

Dawson felt hesitant to hear what she had to say now. She seemed inclined to ruin every notion he ever conceived as reasonable.

"It was - especially for the poor fellow who discovered it."

Sammy cleared her throat again, staving off laughter. "You see, your pre-ancestors were still, more or less, in their primate stage. They were working on important things, such as standing up straight and formulating language. I have to say, that was almost as funny as the fire incident, but, I digress."

"Anyways," She continued, "There was this fellow the rest of the tribe seemed to call Doug, and there was this ritual of courtship that was coming into fashion.

The males would run about with sticks - *special sticks I might add* - of a certain shape and size, and they would go about rubbing these sticks together to make sounds. You know, with the bumps on the sticks. Rudimentary xylophones, you might call them. They made an *awful* racket......

Anyhow, one day Doug, desperate to impress this one female – whose name I have forgotten - figured out that the bumpy sticks made a better sound when the bark was off of them. Now, it just so happened that it was a very dry season that year.

Doug was using one stick to try to work off the rest of the bark from the other stick when all of a sudden; he set fire to the grass in the field!" Sammy Jack started to laugh again. "Then, then - aha ha ha ha! *Oh!*

He's all excited, right? So he goes and tells the rest of the troupe to come see what he did. Of course, the blaze is going wild by that point. They ran like you wouldn't believe!

Burnt down half the savannah, Doug did. And they all got singed too. Just the hair mind you, they didn't really get hurt badly - except maybe their pride. In hindsight, though, it was the first time my kind caught a glimpse of what the future held.

In fact, now that I think of it, I do believe the practice of walking on coals and shamanism came into fashion around about that time as well. Doug was very highly regarded after that. He'd learned to make fire. So I suppose Doug could have also been considered the world's first arsonist. His hair, particularly on his rear end, never did grow back properly. He wasn't a very fast runner you know."

Sammy chuckled as Dawson stared at her in disbelief.

"The caveman who created fire was named Doug?"

"Yes."

"And he set fire to a field…."

"A savannah."

"Sorry, a *savannah*, whilst trying to impress a girl, and that's how fire was created?" Dawson was not overly happy about how insanely idiotic it all sounded.

"Yes, Dawson. That is how it happened. But really, he didn't *create* fire, it already existed. He just learned an alternative way to produce it."

"That's rather disappointing, really." Dawson shook his head.

"What? Well, I guess you don't have the requisite memories to see them play out as they happened, but you can take my word, it was hilarious." Sammy Jack arched her back and stretched.

"It just seems so idiotic." Dawson grumbled as he retrieved his notebook and pen.

Sammy Jack tilted her head. "Tsk. What did you expect Dawson - that a team of primates stood about in a committee and discussed the various methods that might make wood and dry grasses catch fire?"

"I don't know what I expected. I suppose something more profound." Dawson began to scrawl some notes down.

Sammy Jack sighed and shook her head. "That is precisely what I meant before Dawson. Chaos produces unpredictable situations. It is how one chooses to act when those situations arise and what one takes away from them that matters."

She continued. "It took Doug a great deal of effort to reproduce the results he achieved quite by chance. A years' time in fact, but Doug didn't give up. He kept at it for such a long time, the others actually thought he was mad and did everything but shun him.

After he finally managed to figure out a way to get the fire to light predictably, then they all had to learn to control it. Then for generations, the climate was changing, and more of your primordial ancestors had to find ways to produce fire under much more adverse conditions. In fact, it is because of Doug's shenanigans that your whole species survived the ice age. That doesn't make what happened less funny, but, it illustrates that not all discoveries are made by scientific method. Sometimes they are made by accident when an otherwise undesirable male is trying to impress the most desirable female in the group."

Dawson contemplated for a bit. Sammy Jack went back to her grooming as he wrote some more. Suddenly, in the middle of writing Dawson began to laugh.

"What is it?" Sammy Jack looked at him intently.

"A caveman named Doug." Dawson almost choked. He was laughing so hard now that his eyes were wet. "Really?"

Sammy put her paws on his arm. "That was his name…."

"Of course it was Sammy. Of course it was." Dawson took a few deep breaths to calm himself. "I believe you."

"You should. His name really was Doug." Sammy sat back down on the armrest and licked her paw.

Dawson reached over to pet the little cat. "I do believe you…."

Sammy gave Dawson a sidelong look.

"Others might not...." Dawson cracked up laughing again.
"Oh phew." Sammy Jack jumped down off the chair and stalked out of the room, leaving Dawson to finish his writing.

CHAPTER EIGHT

A STROLL IN THE PARK

It is always a nice surprise when a situation which could have turned out to be terrible, in fact, turns out to be quite lovely. That was precisely how Dawson began to feel about his weekend as Sunday afternoon rolled around.

He and Sammy had grown quite close over those few days despite a rough start, and Dawson decided to take Monday off to relax and finish taking notes for the book. After all, why stop when they were on a roll?

In fact, the more Dawson listened to Sammy talk, the more invigorated he had begun to feel.

She had such a whimsical way of looking at the past. Instead of it being series of facts, she told the story of the world in a string of events which were all individual and yet, all connected somehow. Like a string of pearls on a lady's necklace. He and Sammy Jack, needing a break from their dialogue, went for a stroll down to the park.

This, of course, earned an interesting response from all they passed by. How often does one see a man walking with his cat?

When he put himself in their shoes, Dawson almost chuckled to himself. Up until yesterday, he might have thought it curious as well, to see a man walking through the park with a loose cat walking at his heels like a well-trained poodle.

It was a beautiful day to be outdoors, full of sunshine and spring, and one other unexpected thing: Doti Thomas.

She was seated on a park bench, tossing grain to a flock of seemingly ravenous pigeons, when Dawson and Sammy happened across her.

"Doti! Fancy meeting you here today." Dawson grinned broadly.

"Hello! Taking the cat for a walk?" Doti laughed as Sammy jumped into her lap, and bumped her head against Doti's chin affectionately. Doti took Sammy's face playfully between her hands and pressed her nose to the cats. "Now don't you trouble my flock, or I'll be cross."

Sammy responded with a loud mew and Doti let her go.

Dawson chuckled. "I'm sure she will restrain herself, won't you Sammy?"

Sammy sat at the side of the bench as Dawson joined them.

"I'm surprised you don't need her on a leash!" Doti stated with surprise. "She could take off if she sees a dog."

"Oh, she won't." Dawson scratched under Sammy's jaw and she closed her eyes and leaned in. He thought perhaps, he would inquire later as to why she and other animals liked that so much. But then, some things are better left unknown. She enjoyed it. Wasn't that all that mattered?

"So." Doti folded up her now empty bag and set it in her purse, much to the disappointment of the birds, who then eyed the cat with suspicion. "What brought you to the park today?"

"Oh, I don't know." Dawson stretched. "Guess I just needed some fresh air. You know, soak up some vitamin D from all that sunlight."

Doti laughed. "I suppose that's a good idea."

A few moments of silence passed, and they watched the people in the park strolling by. One lady stopped and made a fuss over Sammy, which the cat endured without enthusiasm, causing Dawson to make a few offhanded remarks at Sammy's expense.

"You're looking better than you did on Friday." Doti smiled as she tucked a bit of stray hair behind her ear. "In fact, you seem to be in quite a good mood."

"Oh." Dawson blushed a bit. "Well, I guess I've just had enough rest. And I do love this time of year."

"Me too. Well, I guess you already know that though." Doti looked down at her feet.

"The wildflowers, yes. There's quite a lot come up this year, hasn't there?" Dawson gave Sammy a warning look when she crouched and started to eyeball a bird a bit too closely. Her tail twitched as she sat up again and started to groom as though she had done nothing worthy of note.

"Yes." Doti got this far away look in her eyes. "You know, I never told you, but, when I was little we lived in this big old farmhouse in the countryside. It was surrounded by wildflowers and had a big old apple tree with a swing."

"Sounds lovely." Dawson shuffled his feet.

"Yes. It was." Doti sighed. "I've always longed to go back to that. I don't really like living in the city you know, but, it's where I had to come to work."

"Well, living in town is rather more convenient too, I'd say." Dawson mused. He had never lived in the country but had often heard people talk about their childhoods there. They told of fresh air and swimming holes where all the kids went to cool off in the summer. It was an entirely foreign notion to him.

"I suppose," Doti said a bit sadly. "It doesn't matter. I shall live out the rest of my days in town. Buying a home in the country is very expensive these days."

"You do have this lovely park." Dawson smiled.

"Yes, I do have that." Doti smiled back and their eyes remained locked for just a heartbeat longer than perhaps they should have.

It did not go unnoticed by the cat.

Suddenly, Dawson cleared his throat and looked down at his watch before standing. "Well, um. I should probably... I should get going."

Doti stood too. "Ya. Me too. It was nice to run into you, Dawson."

"Yes. Ah, you too." Dawson shoved his hands in his pockets. "I'll see you at work tomorrow?" Doti touched his arm in a familiar gesture she always seemed to do with him.

"Oh. I'm taking a personal day tomorrow, so, I shan't be there. Tuesday is when I'll be coming in." Dawson shifted his weight.

"Really? I don't think you've ever done that in all the time I've been there." Doti tilted her head, her eyes full of unspoken questions.

"Well, I ah, I got this idea to write a book. So, that's what I've been doing." Dawson looked down at the ground.

"I never took you as a writer Dawson." Doti smiled. "May I read it when it's done?"

"Oh, yes, of course. Who else?" Dawson chuckled.

Doti waved goodbye to him and Sammy before strolling away, casting a few looks back as she left. Dawson turned on his heel with Sammy Jack by his side.

"Well, that was....... awkward." Sammy finally muttered as they walked back in the direction home. "You could have asked her to walk with us for a while."

"Hush Sammy, somebody might hear you." Dawson hissed under his breath.

"Nobody will notice." Sammy rolled her eyes as she trotted alongside Dawson's feet. As if on cue, a little boy's voice perked up from nearby.

"Mummy!!!" The little fellow yelled excitedly, grabbing at his mother's pant leg. "Mummy! That kitty just talked!!!"

The mother brushed him off. "Don't be ridiculous Freddy. Cats don't talk."

She went back to talking on her cell phone. "He says the silliest things sometimes, really. Yes, yes."

Dawson watched the little fellow watching them go as his mother carried on chattering. He felt sorry for the little guy. He had indeed just heard a cat speak. Of course, he would be corrected every time he dared to mention it in the future, and very soon, he would forget it ever happened, to begin with. It would become a hazy memory. A childhood dream, make believe, like an imaginary friend.

"See." Dawson chided again through a discreet hiss.

Sammy Jack turned back towards the little boy and winked, eliciting a huge grin. A chubby little hand waved goodbye as the man and his cat walked away.

A few hours later Dawson was sitting very comfortably in his chair, writing another series of notes from yet another story of mankind's exploits in the Neolithic era. Sammy was in her spot in the window casement, looking out.

"Dawson?" Sammy finally spoke after a long stretch of saying nothing at all.

Dawson looked up from his writing. "Yes, Sammy?"

"Why have you never asked Doti for a date? Is that not what you humans do when you fancy each other?"

"Ehrm, Yes, well." Dawson cleared his throat and blushed crimson. "We're just friends."

"Ah, I see." Sammy Jack gazed out the window as Dawson returned to taking notes. "She's not much good with people either, she told me so herself."

Dawson lost his grip on his pen and it fell from his grasp. "You've spoken with Doti.... I mean....... she knows?"

"No." Sammy Jack looked back again. "She spoke to me. Some humans have a great deal of difficulty talking to each other, so they speak to their pets instead. She spoke a great deal, so I suppose she doesn't say much to other people."

"She talks to me...." Dawson stammered. "We've been friends going on eight years now."

"Oh?" Sammy Jacks mouth almost seemed to tug up at the corners. "What's Doti's favorite color?"

"Lavender. Like the flowers." Dawson picked up the pen irritably.

"She told you that?" Sammy blinked.

"Well, not precisely. But, she always stops when she sees fresh lavender and smells the flowers. And anytime she is picking out something to buy, she always fusses over anything of that color. She also has a lavender plant in her window at her apartment. So; I suppose it's an assumption."

"Very observant of you Dawson." Sammy blinked again.

"What kind of things did she tell you about?" Dawson was now listlessly fidgeting with the writing implement between his fingers.

"Oh, she talked about work, and other times she talked about her dreams," Sammy stated rather blandly, as though it didn't really matter. "You know, that sort of thing. Humans really do get the oddest ideas in their heads."

"Oh." Dawson shuffled some papers around. "Well, what sort of dreams? Like the things she actually dreams about, or, more like what her hopes are for the future?"

"A bit of both, really." The cat's tail swished once, then settled before she turned back to Dawson. "Why don't you ask her? Maybe she'll tell you, and maybe you could tell her some of your own."

Dawson's shoulders dropped a bit. "I don't have any real dreams for the future to share. I have never given it much thought. Not really."

Sammy Jack said nothing, and remained stoic, her eyes directed to the dying light outside the apartment. Dawson was left to the silence of his own thoughts.

He was quite fond of Doti, and they spent more time together then he spent with anyone else. For a long time, he had fancied her. She was a sweet, honest woman, with the kindest heart and the gentlest manner and she never made him feel as though he was less than she was like some people were likely to do. It still made his heart swell a bit every time he saw her. But he had never asked her out.

Dawson had never considered she would be interested in somebody like him. After all, he wasn't very manly. Not all gung-ho and in command like a lot of other fellows. He certainly had no stomach for violence, and he wasn't much for musculature.

"You think she would say yes, to a date? You don't think it would make things....... awkward." Dawson mumbled. He couldn't believe he was discussing his romantic life with his cat. But then, why not? She seemed to know a great deal about everything else.

"Well," Sammy turned back again. "I suppose there is only one way to find out the answer to that." He saw the cat's eyes move towards the hallway, and he followed her gaze to the phone.

If he was honest with himself, in the eight years he had known Doti, he had thought of ringing her for a proper date many times. Simply put, he had never worked up the nerve. Friendship was safe, a relationship was unchartered territory. But really, he thought as he felt his brain shifting gears, there is no such thing as safe.

No certainties, no guarantees, and certainly no refunds when it came to life and the universe. Life held only the promise of something good, but it was he who had the choice whether or not to take it.

"Oh all right then!"

With that, Dawson stood and walked over to the phone. He dialed the numbers and waited, arms crossed, as the phone rang on the other end. Sammy Jack looked on with great interest when Doti's voice came through on the other end.

"Doti?" Dawson stammered nervously.

"Dawson! How are you?" Doti exclaimed merrily, as she always did when Dawson called her. Dawson cleared his throat and turned awkwardly away from Sammy, who was looking quite bemused.

"I was wondering......... did you, um....... well what I mean to say is.......... did you want to maybe try going out sometime?"

There was a pause.

"Well, we often do. What did you have in mind?"

"Well, I thought we might try....... um, well, maybe a nice dinner somewhere?"

There was another brief pause, followed by a melodious giggle.

"I can't believe this, are you asking me out on a date?" Dawson blushed so deeply he thought his cheeks might catch fire.

"Well, um, I thought maybe. We have been friends an awfully long time, and I am quite fond of youuu -*YOUR*- company. I mean, we get along ok right?.......... Well, maybe this wasn't such a good idea......." Dawson's shoulders slouched and he looked a bit frantic as he rambled.

"I would love to Dawson. I really would." Doti's voice was giddy.

"Really?" Dawson's heart was thrumming at a breakneck speed.

"Great! Ya, I will make us a reservation, at, well, I suppose I could make them at the *Blue Rose?*"

"Lovely Dawson. Let me know which evening."

"Of course. I'll see you tomorrow....... I mean, Tuesday, at work... goodnight Doti...." Dawson stammered.

"Good night Dawson." Dawson clicked down the handset and paused a moment before turning back to Sammy grinning ear to ear. "She said yes."

"Fancy that." The cat said in a noncommittal tone. "And to think, it only took eight years......"

CHAPTER NINE

COMPASSION

On Monday morning, after a breakfast of delicious grapefruit marmalade on toast, Dawson decided to go and get the computer he would need to start compiling Sammy's book from all the notes he had taken over the course of the weekend. His mind was full of bits and bobs of information, and he needed to get away to try to decide how he would go about weaving all of it together.

He thought perhaps a trip to the shop would help put things into perspective, but, it didn't quite work out as planned. Dawson came home from the computer shop with several parcels and boxes more than he had intended to get when he went there, and he was feeling quite fatigued from the whole experience. Sammy Jack sat quietly, watching him fumble about with his burden that should perhaps have taken two trips but instead took only a single awkward one.

"I would offer to help, but, for obvious reasons, that is impossible." Sammy stated sympathetically when a few boxes tumbled to the floor.

"Well," Dawson grumbled. "It is the thought that counts."

He managed to get the rest of the lot into the living room and set them on his coffee table.

"Did you buy out the whole store?" Sammy sniffed at the parcels with interest.

"No. Just, it seems that getting a laptop is not such a simple task these days. The salesman kept asking questions and of course, I kept answering. With every question, he seemed to find a different product I needed to have." Dawson plunked down in his armchair and stared at his cargo with disdain.

"Oh?" Sammy was still poking about, sniffing at the boxes.

"Yes. Apparently, one should always have an external hard drive in case the one inside the computer dies so as you don't lose your work. Oh, and a flash drive as well, to transport files more easily. I also had to have a printer, and paper for the printer and an office program for writing. Then I also had to get a surge protector, in case the old wiring in this place caused problems, and wrecked the electronics. I had to have a computer mouse to hook up to the laptop and external speakers because apparently, the speakers built in are not so good. You know, just in case."

Dawson groaned. "I think I've been had......either that or technology is a really big fuss."

"Sounds like a lot of trouble. I must say, I have no real stance on the issue. I am a cat, and we are not so keen on technology. Like most animals, we have no affinity for it. It's a human thing." Sammy, satisfied with her investigation went to the window and jumped up to her usual seat.

"Really? I thought you might know something about it since you seem to know something about most everything else."

"Indeed, but as I've told you, only things which are important to cats. Even when humans were technology-free, we were still friendly with them."

"Here I thought it was just dogs that did that." Dawson stated sardonically.

Sammy looked out the window. "No, it was cats that came first."

"Will you tell me about it? You have never mentioned how that happened." Dawson eyed the pile of boxes and was hoping to have an excuse not to touch them.

"There is not much to tell. But I suppose it can't hurt." Sammy Jack sighed. "See, there was a terrible flood in a small area outside the Nile basin, a very long time ago, even before humans had fire."

"Before Doug's time?" Dawson chuckled.

Sammy chuckled. "Yes, but not too long beforehand, mind. The flood was devastating; many lives were lost, including the mother of some very young kittens. They were not the same kind of cats we are today, but, they were quite similar.

Anyhow, the kittens were alone, starving and grieving for their mother who had been gone for days. It happened that a small group of survivors from a little clan of your ancestors was passing through, trying to find a safe haven from the devastation. Among those was a woman-hunter named Nalah. She heard the kittens crying and went to see what was going on."

"A woman hunter? I thought only men did the hunting?" Dawson interjected.

"Whatever gave you that idea?" Sammy clipped shortly. "Oh yes, the male-oriented establishment of the past few millennia. Well, that was not the way it was back then. It was fairly equal, from what I could tell."

"Oh, I see." Dawson settled back in to hear the rest of what Sammy had to say.

"Now, you must understand, the law of survival was limited to self-preservation, and looking after your own kin. Having satisfied her curiosity, and seeing the kittens orphaned and alone, Nalah left them. She turned away, she had her own worries, and her own people to take care of."

"That's terrible Sammy. She walked away, just like that?" Dawson guffawed.

"Yes, Dawson. Many animals, most, in fact, will. Or they will take advantage of an easy dinner. Nature can be very indifferent you know. It's not all flowers and rainbows, and compassion did not factor into it. Not until that day.

You see, as she walked away from them, something changed in her heart and mind. She turned back you see, she turned back to get them. She took the three little kittens into her care, much to the surprise of her clan. She hunted for them, and cared for them as equally as she did for her own young, and when they could live on their own again, they left, as all feline offspring must do eventually."

Dawson regarded Sammy a moment, feeling a pang of pride. "So that is how we became different than other animals?"

"Yes. It was." Sammy Jack got that faraway look again. "It is what made you appealing. Other animals do use tools. But Nalah's actions changed your whole species. All at once, your fledgling primordial ancestors became what defines you as human, Dawson and compassion and empathy were at the heart of it. She expected nothing in return from those kittens. She simply did what felt right."

"But you said the kittens left when they were grown?" Dawson queried. "So how did you come to be tame?"

"Oh, that was around the same time as the first ice age. It was bitter cold you see, and every creature was suffering from the drastic changes in the climate. The ancestors of Nalahs kittens remembered the human's kindness and sought out shelter with your kind. They let us sleep by their fires, share in their food, and keep their little ones warm from the bitter cold at night. All we needed to do was keep their homes free of pests and show affection towards them once in a while. On the whole, your people were much kinder back then towards other animals and I believe strongly it is at the heart of your species to be as such."

"That's very nice of you to say, Sammy." Dawson smiled warmly.

"It is. Especially considering my lengthy memories which speak to the contrary." Sammy turned her face out the window.

"What about dogs? Is it true that cats and dogs are like oil and water?" Dawson sat up and started to unbox his laptop.

They had helped him set it all up at the store, and installed his software and updates there as well since it would be a few days before his internet was connected.

"Dogs?" Sammy Jack looked back to see what Dawson was doing. "Well, it's like with anyone, some you like, and some you don't. I quite like dogs, personally, even if they forgot how to remember. They are brave, loyal, selfless and kind-hearted unless they are made to be otherwise."

"What do you mean, they forgot how to remember?"

Sammy jack sighed sadly. "Well, it is hard to explain."

"Try me."

"It has to do with love, and how we do it." Sammy shifted.

"Love?" Dawson set aside what he was doing and gave Sammy his full attention.

"Yes. You see, love is love, but every species does it differently. Cats love, but from a distance. Dogs love up close. I believe that is why they chose to forget, it was less painful for them that way."

"What do you mean Sammy?"

"Alongside your ingenuity came a dark and deep capacity for cruelty Dawson - especially for a good-natured creature like my canine counterparts. Dogs and humans are intertwined much more deeply because dogs love up close. They made themselves your self-appointed guardians when you needed it, but it came at a price. So, they stopped remembering all the past transgressions, and the past kindnesses, and the way they came into being, because by the time they saw how things were going to go, it was too late to change their fate."

Sammy Jack turned away. "Sometimes, I wish cats would just forget as well. Maybe someday we will."

Dawson went to her and laid a hand on her back. "I'm sorry Sammy."

"It's all right Dawson." Sammy Jack purred softly. "It wasn't you personally who did any of it. And I have just as many good things to say in defense of humans."

COMPASSION

CHAPTER TEN

A BOOK IS BORN

It was late Friday evening when Dawson arrived back home from his dinner with Doti and he was positively glowing. Sammy met him at the door with her tail held high and rubbed against his legs in greeting.

"Well, how did it go?" She asked after he had taken off his coat and shoes. Dawson smiled in a way Sammy had never seen him smile before.

"Well, it went quite good, Sammy." He walked to the kitchen with the cat on his heels. "In fact, I even brought you something."

"Really? What is it?" Sammy put her paws up on his leg as he pulled a little plastic wrapped package from his pocket and began to open it. He placed the contents on Sammy's plate, a few small pieces of chicken to him, but to Sammy - a buffet.

"Thank you, Dawson!" Sammy dug in straight away, making Dawson chuckle warmly. "Delicious. I could get used to this you know."

"Indeed." Dawson filled the kettle with water and turned on the stove. "It was a lovely evening, couldn't bear to leave you out. So I had them make that special for you. Doti thought it was an awfully good idea as well."

"Of course she did! She has splendid taste." Sammy licked her chops as she finished the last morsel.

"Oh, Sammy! What a lovely time we had. She even held my hand." Dawson looked all misty eyed. "I love her you know. Right from the start, I've loved her. I should have asked her to dinner a long time ago."

Sammy sat back and started to groom her face as Dawson waited on the kettle.

"That's the problem with you humans. You over think things. You needlessly complicate them."

"I suppose," Dawson smirked. "We're meeting at the park again tomorrow, to feed the birds. She asked if I would bring you. You want to come along?"

"Oh yes. I do like to get out of here now and again." Sammy smiled her weird toothy smile again. Dawson tried not to cringe.

The kettle began to whistle and Dawson removed it, pouring the steaming water into his cup and putting in a tea bag. "I think I'll start writing tonight. I know I've been putting it off, but, I think I finally feel up to it."

"You look like you could feel up to anything right now." Sammy trotted out of the kitchen and hopped into the window. Dawson had recently purchased her a mock sheepskin blanket and put it there, much to her delight. Now she kneaded a comfortable spot and lay down to look at the night sky beyond the city lights.

"You know, I always favored the sky at night when I lived out in the country. You could really get a full scope of the vastness outside our planet, the stars are brilliant. Here the lights from the ground choke them out."

Dawson leaned against the casement and followed Sammy's gaze.

"I remember once when my dad took us out fishing. Me and my older brother Lenny, that is. I saw the night sky for the first time without the city lights drowning them out. I got scared and ran into our tent."

With a chuckle, he shook his head. "That was the last time I saw Dad really alive. He loved to go out to the countryside to hunt, or fish, or just roam around. He passed the following September from cancer. Lenny went to college, and me and my mum went to stay with my great aunt Charlotte."

"Oh, you never told me that before," Sammy said sadly. "I'm sorry about that Dawson."

"Nah, it happened a long time ago." Dawson sighed with a sad smile. "We don't get to keep our parents forever."

"Actually you do." Sammy looked back out towards the sky. "That's what memories were made for. The universe wastes nothing, and it forgets nothing. That's one of the beauties of it Dawson."

Dawson decided to change the subject to something less emotional. "I should tell Doti about you. You know, about your ability to talk. It maybe she starts spending a bit of time here."

Sammy Jack shook her head. "I'd prefer you didn't tell anyone Dawson."

"Why not? What's the harm in it?" Dawson raised his brow.

"Please, Dawson. Please promise me you won't tell anyone. It could prove... uncomfortable for you." Sammy sat up and faced him. "What's the harm in people knowing a cat can talk? Maybe that would be a good thing like it was for me. Maybe humans would be kinder to animals if they knew the truth." Dawson pushed.

"What? You mean like the kindly way your species treat each other? You can communicate and yet your kind treats each other like garbage."

Dawson could not really argue with that point. But he did try. "But what about the factory farms and laboratories?"

"Tsk. What about your genocides and wars?" Sammy retorted. "Look, Dawson, if you tell anybody, they will lock you up and throw away the key. They will think you're mad."

"Okay, okay. We will play this your way, Sammy." Dawson smiled warmly and scratched her ear before wandering over to his new desk and opening up the laptop.

He had already transferred all of his notes to it. He just had not set out to make it into something more just yet. There is a point in time when it is time to just do what needs to be done, and that was precisely the moment that Dawson Parks was facing. It was a critical point, one that felt as though it bore a significant bearing on his life, as though he were standing before a great crossroad, and he had only two choices: Go left, or go right.

Until this point - when reality intersected whimsy - Dawson had seen the effort that would be required to actually write the book as some far off concept; a kind of non-reality. It was as though he had been living in a dream and had woken up only to find that the dream had indeed happened, and was not, in fact, a dream at all.

The cat had spoken to him, quite extensively. He was pretty sure he was not having a psychotic episode. In fact, he was enjoying himself immensely this past week. Everything just seemed to be falling into place. For once, Dawson Parks felt like he had a purpose and that feeling of purpose is a very powerful thing indeed. It happens less often than it should for people. It changes them and can mold them into something else entirely. Sometimes that can be a very terrible thing, as Dawson had found out from Sammy's stories, and from history itself. But other times it can do wonders and Sammy Jack made sure he was well aware of that too.

For the first time in his life, Dawson felt both exhilarated and at the same time, completely terrified. His fingers fell to the keys, testing them out a bit with a single sentence, giving the blinking cursor purpose, and also taking the first step on what he knew intuitively, would be a very long journey. Mid-sentence he paused and turned to the cat that was curled up silently by the window, gazing steadily outward. "Sammy?"

"Yes, Dawson?" Sammy Jack did not turn towards him.

CHAPTER TEN

"I think I'd rather like it better if you stayed just as you are."
Dawson stated softly.

Sammy looked back over her shoulder. "Whatever do you
mean?"

"I mean, well, you don't need to go back to being the way
you were before. Not talking." Dawson let out a deep sigh and
turned back to the screen laying his fingers to the keys and
finishing the sentence. "Thank you, Dawson." Dawson smiled
to himself as he finished the first line of the book.

Just because you think something is real doesn't make it real at all.

A BOOK IS BORN

CHAPTER ELEVEN

PARKS AND PROGRESS

The world of Dawson Parks was changing. Not in a way that might be considered noteworthy by most people, but in a way that made a very large difference to him.

Dawson had led a solitary life before; but not for the reasons one might suspect. He was not grievously injured in the heart at some point and driven into a reclusive existence. He was not antisocial, or neurotic. Instead, Dawson was more of a routine oriented person, and he had rather liked it that way. People like Dawson tend to look at life as a long road and one might say that he was living long.

There is another type of person; the person who doesn't always live long, but does live very wide. Those sorts are always about to have another adventure. They were born with an itch that can never be scratched and so they do some of the most unconventional things.

What Dawson began to find, after he came to grips with the notion that a cat could indeed talk - despite all rational arguments to the contrary – that just about anything became possible.

After all, in the event of experiencing the most unlikely scenario, which defies all conventional thought and wisdom, boundaries would matter less wouldn't they? It was a paradigm shift for Dawson.

It took him a full month and many a late night to finish the first draft manuscript for *The Truth About Things According to a Cat*. But when it was finally sent off to the freelance editor he had hired, an enormous weight seemed to lift off Dawson's shoulders.

The book was nearly finished, he had all but made good on his agreement with Sammy Jack. Every evening, as long as the weather agreed, Sammy and Dawson took a stroll through the park. If the weather did not agree, they would sit in and watch TV together.

It was a unique and different situation from what most people might experience with their pets, but then again, maybe only the talking made it different.

Sammy was still a cat, very much so in fact. But she was a cat that could be understood and answer back. It became very apparent to Dawson, as he watched other people interact with their own companion animals, that most folks thought very little of the intelligence of other creatures.

There were those few who didn't, but, all in all, human beings lacked consideration towards them. They yanked hard on leashes, yelled at them, ignored them, and carried on about what a pain they were and how they wished they had never had them.

It was all just a misunderstanding, really. If the animals could explain their side of things, perhaps their custodians would go easier on them.

Dawson had never treated Sammy Jack unfairly. With the exception that before she decided to communicate, he had never considered she might like to get outside for the occasional stroll.

He had noticed a few other cat owners take to the same routine as he had over the past few weeks, although their cats were of course on harness and lead.

Doti was also becoming a bigger and bigger part of their lives. The three of them had started to have adventures together. Nice adventures, like the time Dawson rented a car for the day and taken Sammy and Doti out to the countryside for a picnic. Sammy had chased frogs and grasshoppers and stalked birds all afternoon, whilst Dawson and Doti strolled along winding trails.

Then, beside a little pond Doti - tired of waiting - had planted a kiss right on Dawson's lips - *their first kiss* - much to his surprise and delight.

Another adventure on a Saturday afternoon involved an elderly lady named Doris Kingsley, who had lost her dog. They had spent hours going around the park calling for the dog — only to realize later that he was, in fact, a stuffed toy who was 'hiding out' by the water fountain.

When Doti asked Mrs. Kingsley about it, she had smiled sweetly, holding the wayward plush in her arms.

She said: "I found him in a corner shop one day. He reminded me so much of my old dog Rodney, and I just had to have him. I'll never have another dog, you see. It wouldn't be fair; I'm far too old for it now. But, I do like to have this little fellow along. I suppose that all sounds quite foolish."

"Not at all. It sounds just fine to me." Doti had reassured her.

Sammy Jack had said right at the beginning that life was a portrait, and that the universe was the artist, but that we were all the writers of our own stories within it. Dawson was beginning to see how very true that was with every person he opened his world up to include and he was watching where he was going for once.

The road ahead looked full of possibility and promise.

A few weeks after the manuscript was sent via email to the editor, it arrived back and Dawson printed out the second, edited, hard copy of it to keep on record. The editor had expressed his gratitude at having been chosen to edit the book and had enjoyed reading it very much. Dawson enjoyed the lack of editing he had to do and thanked the editor very much in turn.

"So is it ready?" Sammy sat on the living room table.

"It looks that way Sammy. It's edited and ready for print. Now we just have to find a publishing house crazy enough to take it."

Flipping through the hardcover pages, he couldn't believe the scope of what he had written, or that he had been able to write such an enormous telling from front to back at all.

Of course, he hadn't done it alone. Sammy had told him all the facts and had been quite forthcoming whenever he got stuck.

"Somebody will take it. You did a very nice job on it, Dawson. Better than I would have thought, although I am no literary critic." Sammy stretched and yawned. "So, what happens now?"

"Well, I'll be sending out a bunch of samples to various publishing companies." Dawson opened his laptop to check his emails. He had come to enjoy having a laptop at home and had started to become quite accustomed to using it, even if it was an extra expense.

Now that the book was completed, he mostly just used it to chat with Doti and a few of his other friends on social media.

"And then?" Sammy pressed.

"We wait to either be accepted or, rejected." Dawson sighed.

He had already composed all the electronic forms for the publishing companies, and the freelance editor he had hired to prepare the manuscript had also prepared his samples for submission in the proper format for each.

The whole process had cost Dawson a pretty penny, but for Sammy's sake, it was worthwhile. That the little cat had no real sense of commerce touched Dawson most deeply of all.

She had no motives to become wealthy or famous. She simply had the idea that she might like a story shared, and had asked for his assistance. There was a purity of purpose there that made Dawson not blink an eye when he spent a good deal of his savings making it possible.

He had become much less miserly over the past little while and was even considering moving to a newer apartment.

It was nearly eight weeks later, and a shoebox worth of rejection letters when Dawson finally received an envelope that made him take the stairs two at a time. "Sammy!"

He called as he raced into the apartment. "Sammy, we've been accepted!"

"Really?" Sammy jaunted out of the bedroom and sniffed the letter when Dawson held it down for her.

"Yes. It says right here: We are pleased to inform you that we are prepared to accept your manuscript for print!" Dawson grinned broadly.

"That's wonderful Dawson! When will we get to see it?" Sammy purred happily.

"Oh, a while yet. But isn't it wonderful Sammy! You'll be published....... under my name of course, but what a grand achievement for a little cat."

Dawson scratched her ears excitedly. "Does it make you happy?"

"Oh, Dawson." Sammy leaned against his hand as he scratched her neck. "I have always been happy. I didn't need any paper to tell me to be so. But I am pleased."

Another two months would pass before the book went to print and October had put a chill into the air, warning that winter was soon to come. Doti was visiting when Dawson received the book in the mail, and because she was still oblivious to Sammy's ability to talk, Sammy of course had to restrain herself.

That proved especially difficult when Dawson pulled out the hardcover first edition. Sammy's picture was right on the front. A beautiful portrait print Dawson had commissioned to send into the publishing house to be used in the title. Over a clanging of glasses, Dawson and Doti toasted the book as Sammy looked over the cover with great interest.

Dawson opened the book to the dedication. Inside it said: *To Sammy Jack, if not for you, this book would not have been possible.*

PARKS AND PROGRESS

CHAPTER TWELVE

THE TROUBLE WITH SUCCESS

There are people who seek to do the inspired, and then there are those who simply do it without seeking it at all.

Dawson had never conceptualized a story in his whole life. He didn't read anything but the newspaper recreationally, and he never daydreamed. Nothing inspired him to see anything beyond what he did each day, and what he planned carefully to achieve for his retirement.

The in-between was just filler.

Because of this, he had never felt the despair that can accompany aspiration, never felt denied what he should have done, or should have had. He had lived a comfortable life, a nondescript one, with very little stress, and absolutely no complication.

That is until he brought home Sammy Jack and she flipped everything around with the simple act of talking with him.

His life was less simplistic now, and it became even more complicated when he decided to take a chance inviting Doti into the mix as well.

Dawson had found joy, and joy as easy as it may appear to come across, is not in fact. He still had a relatively uncomplicated life, but now, there was joy. And something else as well - an email from his agent which read in all caps: U WILL NOT BELIEVE THIS!

Dawson smirked as he looked at Sarah Wally's subject title. He couldn't believe that a literary agent would put down U in place of YOU. "Tsk tsk Sarah."

He chuckled to himself as he opened her message. It was now cold and rainy outside more often than sunny, the months had flown by and the days were growing colder daily.

Dawson always found November to be a rather odd time of year, being neither autumn nor winter despite its classification. He kind of thought of it more in terms of being a limbo transition between the seasons, where on the streets everyone referred to time as nearly Christmas.

But it wasn't anything, just a phase one had to pass through, and the weather -of course - was as awful.

Dawson had to read the email message a few times through but it still wouldn't seem to register in his brain - something about his book jetting abruptly into the best sellers list.

He closed the lid of his laptop, walked into the kitchen, got another cup of coffee, sat back down and stared at the chrome lid for a few moments. The book had only been out for a month, so, he knew he must have read Sarah's email wrong.

"Doti." He called out.

"What is it?" She responded from the bedroom. Waiting on her coffee like usual, Dawson smiled inwardly, and Sammy Jack would no doubt, still be curled up by her legs.

Doti spent a great deal of time at his place now, and he had grown very accustomed to her presence, despite his many years of bachelorhood.

"Could you come look at something for me, pet?" Dawson called back; he was still staring at the closed lid.

Doti wandered out of the bedroom in her teddy bear pajama bottoms and matching top. Dawson had given the set to her for her birthday in August since she always seemed so set on ogling every plush teddy bear they came across in the shops.

"What is it?" Doti pushed her messy hair back behind her ears and sat down next to him. Dawson leaned back on the couch and pointed at the laptop. "There's an email there from Sarah. I don't think I read it right. Take a look will you?"

"Well, what'd you close the lid for? Silly." Doti smiled and gave him a playful shove before she opened the lid again. The screen flickered back to life and she leaned forward and read the email. Then she read it again, a little closer this time, as she was not wearing her glasses.

Finally, her breath caught and she exclaimed. "Oh my god!"

"I guess I read it right......." Dawson exhaled deeply; he hadn't realized he had been holding his breath until just then.

"Oh my *GOD!*" Doti looked it over again. "Dawson! I can't believe it... I can't... A book tour she says? And she's asking when you'll start working on another......"

"Ya. I'm not doing that. Not in my contract. I'm not doing it." Dawson grumbled.

"Why not Dawson? You wrote the book; one would think you'd be happy that it is so popular." Doti's face was full of confusion, naturally.

He should have been happy with the results, but instead, he suddenly felt quite frustrated instead. A sense of dread seemed to have taken hold of his emotions.

"I know. I honestly didn't think anyone would read the thing Doti......... it was supposed to be a....... Oh! Never mind."

Dawson stalked over to the window and crossed his arms, looking out at the rain. He felt sick to his stomach.

"Dawson, you know, most authors do tend to promote their books....... here look, she says all expenses paid." Doti tried to sound reassuring.

"I don't care about any of that. I don't want to go meet a bunch of strangers like that, sign books and talk about the thing." Dawson snarked. "That's not who I am."

"You know, for someone who just achieved something quite grand, you're being very crass." Doti crossed her arms and looked at him with a disapproving eye. "I don't know what's bothering you Dawson, but it's quite the mood swing you've taken all of a sudden. Don't do the tour then, it's your career."

"My career is at the bank. I like my job." Dawson didn't look at her.

Doti closed the lid of the laptop. "I've got to get ready for work. I'm sorry you're so disappointed your book is such a success."

"Right." Dawson muttered. Doti started to walk to the bedroom but paused in the doorframe. Sammy Jack was stretching and yawning behind her on the bed. "You know, some people work their whole lives, pour everything they have into having just a glimpse of what you've achieved in what? A month? You should consider that before you go around telling anyone else how unhappy you are with it."

Dawson didn't answer her; he just turned away again to look at the rain splattering on the window sill. He heard the familiar thud of Sammy's feet hitting the wooden floor as she dropped off the bed, followed by a tap tap tap as she made her way towards him.

Doti closed the door and he heard the radio turn on in the room. She tended to like to listen to the radio as she sorted herself for the day.

"What was all that?" Sammy whispered, jumping up into the casement and sitting before him.

"You know; I wish you would reconsider keeping your talking a secret from Doti. We may very well move in together someday, and I'd rather she knew what she was getting into." Dawson snapped at her in hushed tones.

"Well, you're in a mood aren't you?" Sammy started to groom herself.

"The book is a success Sammy. Now they want me to do a book tour, and signing and readings and interviews." Dawson sighed, placing his hands against the wall and leaning his forehead against them. The anxiety of that thought had him twisted up in knots.

"That's good isn't it Dawson? You humans do so like your notoriety, and this should put you up a few rungs on that ladder." Sammy carried on grooming, pausing only to talk.

"I didn't set out to climb any ladders, Sammy, and I'm not especially fond of being of interest to anyone outside my circles. Besides, I didn't really write the book." Dawson groaned. "It was supposed to just be a bit of fun."

"You wrote that book, Dawson. I just told you a bunch of facts, but you truly are a poet at heart." Sammy looked at him with feline admiration.

"They want me to write another now."

"So write another" Sammy looked out the window.

"I didn't set out to write books for a living, Sammy. I'm happy to just be a bank teller." Dawson turned and leaned his back against the wall. "Besides which: What shall I write? I have no idea!"

"So be a bank teller. Dawson, I don't see why you are getting so worked up." Sammy Jack jumped down off the sill and trotted towards the kitchen. "How about some breakfast? It always makes you feel better when you serve me food."

"Right. We'll have to talk about that." Dawson exhaled sharply and followed the cat into the kitchen. "I suppose I should apologize to Doti too."

"Yes. That would be wise if you wish her to stick around. I know I certainly do." Sammy turned in circles around his feet as he opened her tin, and emptied it into her dish.

He took out a fork and mashed it a bit before he set it down for her.

"You know; you should really try some of this someday. It's very good." Sammy spoke between mouthfuls.

"I'll keep that in mind." Dawson gave the smelly food a grim appraisal.

"Well, if I were you, Dawson, I would approach this situation like a cat." Sammy paused a moment and licked her chops.

"Oh? How's that?" Dawson raised a brow.

"Ignore it and perhaps it will go away." Sammy went back to eating.

Dawson ran his hands through his hair. "I tried that once......... didn't really work out."

CHAPTER THIRTEEN

CRITICAL VELOCITY

Lessons can be very easy to understand, yet very difficult to learn - especially the lesson of *Ignoring a problem doesn't make it go away*.

That is unless you are a cat. Cats get away with quite a lot in regards to breaking universal laws, but then, maybe universal laws don't apply to all creatures the same way. It's not fair, and you could lodge your complaints to the celestial powers that settle these things but the likelihood of anything being done about it is minimal.

After all, the universe and all of its workings are very complex, and it's unlikely it will redefine itself simply to satisfy you.

This did not stop Dawson from making a vain attempt at trying to ignore his situation, much to the chagrin of his publicist.

To see it from Dawson's perspective, though, you would have to accept that fame does not equal freedom – not to everyone. For Dawson, it was something more likened to a gilded cage threatening to swallow his new found liberty at any moment.

The book was everywhere; it had even been released in stocking stuffer size for Christmas time and was available as an eBook for tablets and readers. The real problem was this; everywhere the book was, so too was Dawson's face.

Now most people might not have recognized Dawson from the photograph on the *About the Author* page, but there was always that *one*. That one person in question is precisely what lead up to an uncomfortable experience for Dawson at work one snowy afternoon, six days after New Years.

He had just finished assisting an older lady who had her overly snoopy sister in tow.

"Dawson." The woman scrutinized Dawson's name tag for a moment while adjusting the fit of her glasses.

"Oh *my!* Liddy, that's *Dawson Parks!*"

Dawson felt his face flush a bit red as the woman tugged at her sister's arm.

"Well, my word!" Said her sister, Liddy. The woman drew a book – his book- from her bag and Dawson knew he was found out. "It is him! I knew I recognized you! From this picture on the back sleeve, see?"

The woman held up the photo in the open book to show Dawson, as though he weren't aware of what he looked like.

"Yes... that's me." He laughed nervously as a few more patrons and his co-workers started to become distracted by the scene.

"I didn't know you worked for the bank." Liddy stated, as though the idea was somehow an odd concept.

Dawson wondered if people realized that even authors had to pay bills. "Um, uh yes. Going on ten years now."

He cleared his throat and tried to look like he had something pressing to attend to on his computer screen.

"Well, my sister and I have just been reading that book of yours! Splendid! Simply darling. I just loved it." The woman put her book on the counter, and the sister added her own, only half-read copy judging from the bookmark.

CHAPTER THIRTEEN

"Thank you. That's …. uh……. that's great." Dawson shifted his weight nervously.

Attention had been drawn from other patrons in the cue. He wasn't enjoying this.

"Would you please sign our copies dear?" The woman asked. "I've never had a book signed by the author before."

"Sure, no problem…." Dawson cast an uncertain gaze in the direction of his boss, Henry, who was now observing the interaction from Doti's booth.

It was a very uncomfortable situation indeed, especially with his employer looking on. He humored the ladies and signed their books, hoping to get rid of them.

"Oh thank you so much! What a nice young man you are."

The woman sounded almost giddy as she turned to her sister. "Just wait until I tell everyone at the book club!"

They left quickly, laughing and chattering excitedly.

Dawson let out a heavy sigh and turned to the cue. "Next?"

Fifteen people rushed to see him, books in hand. "One at a time! Oh, it's the book? No no, I can't.…"

Dawson was trying to talk over the symphony of requests, but they weren't listening. Dawson felt ill. This wasn't supposed to happen at work. Henry sighed and shook his head as he made his way towards Dawson.

He placed a firm hand on his shoulder. "Come on, we'd best get you out of here Dawson."

They walked past the offices and went out the staff door at the back of the building. Doti quickly caught up, her expression grave.

The trio walked in silence towards the next street. Obviously, the fans hadn't known where to look for them, although they all took turns keeping an eye out.

"I suppose I'll have to put in my resignation, Henry. Sorry." Dawson said sheepishly, as he hailed a taxi.

"No worries Dawson. I knew this was coming when that book of yours got so popular. Didn't take long either." Henry clapped his shoulder. "But damned if we won't miss you around here. We'll keep in touch."

"I wasn't expecting any of this Henry. I didn't even expect anyone would read the bloody thing. Now it's going to print in North America too in the next few months." Dawson opened the taxi door then turned back to shake Henry's hand. "I really am sorry."

"Ah, never mind that. It was a decent read. Not my thing really, to be honest, but, seems a lot of folk like the idea of a cat telling the history of the world. Ha ha! Imagine that." Henry pulled Dawson in for a quick hug. "Good on you Dawson. Now, get out of here before they find you."

"See you later love." Doti leaned in and gave him a kiss goodbye.

The cab pulled away and the ride home was uncomfortable and anxious. Dawson had been happy these past months with Sammy and Doti, and the little world they had built.

All of a sudden, he was becoming the hot topic of discussion.

According to the commentaries in local and national media, he had come out of nowhere to be on the top seller's list and was quite the enigma.

Dawson of course, was not trying to be mysterious by refusing public appearances – he was simply trying to pretend none of it was happening. Being the center of attention made Dawson very uncomfortable. He didn't want to be in the limelight; he didn't want to be in the lemon light or the orange light either.

They could keep those lights to themselves, thank you very much.

Now there were demands for another book on top of everything else. A sequel, they wanted! How was he to manage that? It wasn't even his story, it was Sammy's. She deserved the credit, not he. But then, she wouldn't even let him tell Doti about her unique disposition.

Instead of going straight home, he asked the cabbie to drive around the city for a while; after all, why not? He seemed to have come into affording such frivolities. The book was all over the place; in every shop window of every bookstore and his bank balance had now nearly hit the six figures mark.

CHAPTER THIRTEEN

It was not that he hated it, not precisely, but it all felt very alien to him at the same time. It was as though another man's life had come along and shoved his aside. A few hours and a sizeable cab fee later, he was sitting on the couch at home watching the television with Doti.

Sammy Jack lay dozing in his lap as they drank wine and watched *The Good, The Bad, and The Rating.* A show Doti announced earlier was covering his book.

Paul Harriot, the host of the show, and a cynic if ever there was one, sat on the couch of the studio alongside his guests; Mina Faye, a well-known crime novelist, and Bartley Knight, the host of another television series on the same network: *Late Nights with Knight.*

Paul smirked and huffed when they came around to discussing the book. "That book is the kind of literary drivel that I absolutely despise."

Bartley Knight leaned back in his seat, raising his eyes in over emphasized surprise. "Well, surely you must like something about it, Paul. I mean, it seems to have made quite the impression on the readers."

Paul sneered. It made his face look a bit like a weasels, although Dawson was sure a weasel would take offense to that idea. He never watched Harriot's show because he couldn't stomach the man's negativity at the best of times.

"Of course it has." Stated Paul with disgust. "It's positively *dripping* with pop philosophy. Makes me sick. Just the premise of it. I mean who would think of telling a story like that?"

Rolling his eyes, he continued. "It's absolute rubbish."

"Well, I hate to disagree with you, Paul...." Mina Faye interjected and then added very cleverly. "Well actually, I love to disagree with you...."

The audience chuckled and there was some scattered clapping of hands as she cast a well-practiced smile in their direction. "But I quite enjoyed it. It was honest, and I think the author has a lovely grasp of symbolism."

Dawson shifted and grumbled to himself as Sammy watched the show intently. "Bunch of foolishness. Imagine if they knew the truth of it, Sammy? Imagine that. Symbolism. Good heavens."

Doti looked over at Dawson where he sat brooding. "Dawson, it really worries me sometimes when you talk to that cat like she can understand you."

"Sorry love." Dawson sank deeper into his chair, feeling dark clouds gathering overhead, and his mood was a direct reflection of it. Sammy gave him a curious look but said nothing - as usual when Doti was around.

"Yes. Myself as well Mina." Bartley Knight chimed in, inviting another rude eye roll from Paul Harriot. "My daughter especially loved it. The cat, you see?"

The studio burst into laughter, save for Paul Harriot, who maintained his crass demeanor. "Bollix, the lot of it. I swear the literary world is spiraling the drain. They will put just about anything to print these days. And what's more...."

Dawson was roused by the ringing of the telephone. He turned down the volume and picked up the handset in the hallway as Doti and Sammy Jack carried on watching the program. "Hello?"

"Dawson! I have the most amazing news! You won't believe it!" It was Sarah Wally, his literary agent. A young woman whose fledgling career had been made through representing him. For that, he knew she would be eternally grateful, even if he kept telling her it was no big deal.

Doti looked over in his direction and he mouthed Sarah towards her.

"Oh! Hello, Sarah!" Doti called from the couch and waved as if Sarah could actually see her.

Sarah and Doti had become fast friends, and it worked out rather well. Sarah did almost all the talking and Doti hardly did any at all.

"Oh, hello Doti!" Sarah yelled into the phone, making Dawson wince away from the handset.

Doti shrugged apologetically; Dawson sighed. "What's so amazing?"

Sarah's tone was abnormally high-pitched in her excitement.

"Bartley Knight's assistant Laurence just called me to book an impromptu interview with you on Friday night! They're shooting at the studio in town here, so, you won't even need to travel. Isn't that wonderful?!"

"I don't know if I want to Sarah…." Dawson felt his stomach churn. It would be national television, even if it was late at night. People would be watching it for sure, Bartley Knight was so popular.

"Come on Dawson. I've let you weasel out of a great deal, but, you need to help me out here." Sarah sounded a bit stressed by his refusal.

"Sarah, you didn't……." He turned to the television.

"I did……. sort of jump the gun." Sarah sounded even more strained.

Dawson turned up the volume a bit, just in time to hear Bartley Knight's announcement: "And it seems we will be having Dawson Parks himself on Late Nights this Friday, so be sure to stay tuned."

"Sarah!" Dawson exclaimed, mortified. "You said yes?"

"I……. got a bit excited. Sorry. But Dawson, it's *Bartley Knight!*" Sarah's voice carried a tremble in it. He could have fired her for that, but then Doti would be angry with him and he would be angry with himself for it as well.

"Okay………. okay. I'll do the blasted interview, Sarah." Dawson grumbled, running his fingers across his brow. "Oh, thanks, Dawson! Have a good night. Tell Doti I'll text her!" The line went dead, and Dawson hung up.

Doti looked at him, eyes questioning. Dawson exhaled sharply. "Looks like I am doing an interview with Bartley Knight."

She stood and walked over to him, putting her arms around his waist as he reciprocated the action. "Are you going to be able to handle it, Dawson? I know you don't want to…."

"I haven't much choice now do I, hun?" Dawson laid his forehead against Doti's. "I'll be fine. I just wasn't expecting any of this."

"I'll go make some tea." Doti placed a quick kiss on his cheek and left him to go to the kitchen. Dawson went to his armchair, which had become his sanctuary as of late, and Sammy jumped up in his lap. He patted her head. "What have you gotten me into Sammy Jack, you silly cat." Sammy didn't answer, lest Doti hear her, but instead bumped her forehead against Dawson's chin and did her freakish cat smile.

"I really wish you wouldn't do that." Dawson groaned.

"Were you saying something, Dawson?" Doti called from the kitchen.

"No hun! Just the telly." Dawson laid his head back and closed his eyes. His stomach tensed in knots. How am I to manage this?

CHAPTER FOURTEEN

LATE KNIGHT

The hustle and bustle of backstage melted away into a sudden silence as Dawson was escorted and practically shoved into a place the staff casually referred to as the green room.

His first thought was probably the same thought that most folk unfamiliar with show business would have; why do they call it the green room? After all, it wasn't actually green at all. In this case, it was a pasty looking pale gray, with a couch, a coat rack and a vanity which housed a brightly lit mirror.

"Now Dawson, uh, Dawson......?" Frank, who was an assistant of some sort tried to get Dawson's attention. "Hey, focus here."

Dawson's nerves were wound so tight he thought he might lose his supper if he had bothered to eat any at all.

"Ya, of course. What is it, Fred?"

"Frank..." The blond haired youth sighed, it was only the fourth time Dawson had got his name wrong.

"Right, sorry." Dawson made his way over to the couch and sat with his head in his hands. "I can't bloody do this......"

"You don't have a choice now. Besides, it's not so bad! The lights are so bright; you'll hardly see the audience." Frank tried to fake reassurance, although Dawson was fairly certain he thought Dawson was an idiot.

"That's not what I mean...," Dawson grumbled.

Frank rolled his eyes. "Look, just try to calm down. You're on in fifteen. Remember what we rehearsed?"

Dawson nodded. "Good. Don't forget. And if you're going to throw up, do it before you go on stage."

Frank nudged a small trash bin towards him and Dawson gave him an incredulous glare. "I'll leave you to it."

Frank looked down towards his clipboard and rushed from the room, leaving Dawson alone. After a few moments passed, Doti was let into the room. A stage pass hung on a loop from her neck.

"Phew! They're a busy lot back here aren't they?!" She grinned and exhaled, plopping down beside him on the couch.

"Yah." Dawson lay back, crossing his arms. His eyes moved about the room, not focusing on one thing or the another.

Doti placed a reassuring hand on his arm. "Is there anything I can do to help make this easier?"

Go back in time and tell me not to publish that book? He thought miserably.

"No." Dawson closed his eyes, trying to block out the reality which was eminent. He was going on national television and it was too late to back out now.

Doti took his hands. "Dawson look at me." He did as she asked, and she leaned in, placing her forehead against his. "When you're out there, don't think of the people in the audience, just think of it like...... like you're at the bank and that Bartley Knight is just another patron."

Dawson kissed her and pulled away. "I wish it were that easy......."

"It is that easy. If you let it be." Doti's voice was full of concern.

"But it shouldn't even be me out there........." Dawson's voice trailed off.

CHAPTER FOURTEEN

"Of course it should. You wrote a fantastic book, Dawson." Doti smiled so sweetly. He could see it there; the absolute pride in her eyes. She was proud of him, and that pride made this whole thing even worse.

It came to him quite suddenly, the reason he was so troubled about the whole situation. It was one thing to take credit where credit is due; Dawson had no problem with that. But what had happened, what he had done, was take credit for someone else's dream, someone else's gift.

He felt as though he were a thief, even though Sammy Jack didn't see it that way. The whole thing felt incredibly wrong and he desperately needed to set it right.... at least with her.

"Doti....... there, there's something you ought to know......." Dawson squeezed her hands. "I should have told you.... but...."

"Time to go Dawson." Frank leaned into the room, tapping his watch impatiently. Doti looked confused.

"You see, it's about Sammy....." Dawson tried to explain further.

"What about Sammy? Is she okay?" Doti looked alarmed now. He was doing this all wrong.

"Dawson! Hey, come on mate! *Time.*" Frank groaned impatiently.

Dawson shook his head in frustration. "I'll tell you after....... promise."

"Okay..." Doti let his hands go as he stood and followed Frank from the room. There was no turning back now.

Little known to Dawson was that two very concerned golden eyes were fixed upon the television set in his living room, as he awkwardly entered stage right. Bartley Knight, the famous host of *Nights with Knight Live*, stood and shook hands with a very uncertain looking Dawson Parks before they both took their designated seats.

The crowd went wild, cheering and whistling and carrying on as Sammy Jack watched Dawson do his best impression of looking at ease. It was not convincing.

In fact, the man looked like a nervous wreck.

"Just smile Dawson, and don't say anything foolish." Sammy Jack whispered, repeating what she had told Dawson earlier.

He had left the television on for her before he left the apartment, so she could watch the broadcast if she wanted too. Now that she saw him on stage, she felt very concerned over her human friend.

You see, there are some people who are born very interesting, and there are those who – with great effort -become very interesting.

People, who are born interesting, are not generally reliant on genetics, but instead, association; such as a princes or princess, or the child of a Hollywood star. Occasionally they are born into it in a less positive way, but more often than not, it is by one of the aforementioned means.

People who - through their own efforts - become interesting, tend to do so over a long period of time.

Whichever way it works out, they become accustomed to the attention and scrutiny of others- positive or negative - as it has always been a part of their lives. They tend to become interesting simply by default because it is expected of them.

The ones who unexpectedly fall into being interesting, well, that is another situation altogether.

It is one thing to be popular or not, amongst one's peers. It is another thing to suddenly be in the spotlight of a nation, which was precisely what Dawson had stumbled into. He clearly wanted nothing to do with it.

"Yes, yes! Very good!" Bartley Knight grinned broadly and gestured for the crowd to settle. It was a practiced gesture, and one his guests and viewers were well acquainted with, as they began to quiet down immediately.

Turning his attention to Dawson, he leaned his elbows onto the polished surface of his desk, clasping his hands before him.

"Well, welcome to the show Mr. Parks, or shall I call you Dawson?"

Dawson cleared his throat. "Dawson should be just fine. Thank you."

The crowd gave an appreciative round of applause before settling again.

"So, this book...." With that, Knight moved his hands to pick up a book from his desktop and lifted it for the crowd to see the cover. The viewers started hooting and whistling and clapping again.

Dawson grinned nervously, and even with the lower quality resolution of the television set, Sammy could see he was sweating.

Knight let the book slide backward and forward, in his idle grasp, almost as though he were fanning the crowd.

"This book, which I am quite sure everyone in this audience has read." *More cheering, more applause.* "This is – well - this is the silliest book I think I have ever read."

Laughing and chortling erupted from the crowd but stifled quickly.

"Well. I suppose it would seem rather silly......." Dawson stuttered, wringing his hands together in his lap and smiling again at the home audience.

"Yes. Yes indeed." Knight grinned broadly. "It is a very humorous read. I mean the very idea of a cat telling history. I don't think I have ever laughed so hard in all my life."

"Oh, yes. Right." Dawson swallowed hard.

"A bit nervous, being here tonight?" Bartley Knight smirked and did his best impression of being concerned. It was convincing.

"Oh, yes. A bit." Dawson let out a sharp sigh, and the crowd chuckled. "Sorry, I'm just not used to all this.

"Indeed, indeed." Knight nodded. "So, when did you begin writing, Dawson? Or, when did you decide to be a writer?"

"Well." Dawson licked his lips. "Well, I suppose it all started when my......... I mean when *I* started taking down notes, for the book. Then I knew I would have to write it, so, I did. I wrote it, I mean."

"Did you write stories when you were a child? I would imagine you were quite the storyteller as a boy." Knight leaned forward and grinned his star quality smile.

"Not really, no." Dawson shifted about until he found another, more comfortable position.

Sammy Jack moved closer to the television screen, almost as though trying to get closer to her friend. "Steady on now Dawson."

"So you just, what, out of the blue got this idea to write this fantastically silly account of history, through the eyes of a cat?"

Knight leaned back incredulously.

"Well, I didn't really feel I had much of a choice, once she got going." Dawson laughed anxiously and so did the audience and his host.

Knight leaned forward again, sharp as a knife; he'd caught the slip-up.

"Oh no." Sammy's heart dropped. Dawson was losing his nerve, he was terrible at lying at the best of times, but put under stress... Dread filled the little cat's mind as to what would inevitably happen next.

"Once *she* got going?" Knight smiled wickedly. "Was there a secret co-writer Dawson? A lovely lady moonlighting as a muse perhaps?"

"Oh, no! Nothing like that, I was talking about the cat!" Dawson exclaimed before his mind caught up to his mouth.

"The....... *cat?*" Knight sat back, his brow raised in surprise.

Dawson's eyes went wide for a moment as he realized what he had said, but then, much to his own mortification – he continued.

"Yes, well. What I meant was, uh, err, well, it was her idea, and she wouldn't stop...... so, well, I did technically write it...... on her behalf. After all, she can't type. She lacks the adequate phalanges."

The studio was dead silent before erupting wildly with laughter.

"Good lord Dawson, you almost had me going there!" Barnaby Knight was laughing loudly, matching the tempo of the audience.

Dawson shifted uncomfortably, his eyes downcast, his face humorless. Then, all of a sudden, and at the worst possible moment, he decided to be bold, if not downright righteous. He was tired of claiming credit for something he didn't do. It was Sammy's brilliance, not his; he'd just done a bunch of typing.

"It's true. It *was* my cat's idea!" Dawson's face went a few shades of crimson as the crowd went silent once more. His voice was a bit broken, but firm. Jittery, but determined. He proceeded. "You see, I mean, what you need to understand is, just because you think something is real, doesn't make it real at all."

"The first line in your book." Knight had his turn to look a bit uncomfortable now; his eyes glanced towards the backstage for a moment.

"Yes. That bit was mine and a few others. But the book was a request from Sammy Jack, my cat." Dawson trembled as another realization dawned on him, and it sat heavy and humbling on his shoulders.

He had to keep going now. "See, I've never amounted to anything much. Never had an idea in my life, worth repeating – until I brought Sammy home. Not even as a child. I'm not the sort of person that has a big or interesting existence. All I ever did was live in a box. Until I got this cat and she changed everything. She opened up my eyes to so much more, to the idea that maybe someone as mundane as myself could do interesting things. Be something, well, *more*. Someone *different*. She didn't save my life, but she gave me one and for that, I shall be eternally grateful. Sammy is not just *my cat*, she's my friend."

If a cat had the capability of tears, the little ginger cat might have shed a few. "Awe Dawson. You sod. Now you've done it."

The studio was dead silent.

"Right, well. I think it's time for a commercial break." Knight cued the camera man and the show cut out quite suddenly, and in a way that made Sammy very uncomfortable. The Posh Kitty Kibble Quartet came on screen in all their animated glory and began to strut about in sync, singing the praises of their brand.

The minutes crawled on like years as Sammy waited for the talk show to come back on, and when it finally returned, the show proceeded without Dawson.

In his stead, Bartley Knight was beckoning the next guest, a famous comedian Ricky Finlay, onto the stage.

"Oh, no......" Sammy Jack paced around the flat, uncertain of what to do. An hour passed, then another. Dawson had yet to return home.

The phone rang, and Sammy knew instinctively she would have to try to answer it. She leaped up onto the table and pawed at the handset until it fell off the receiver and dangled precariously over the edge.

"Hello, Sammy?" It was Dawson's voice, and he sounded a bit distressed. "Dawson! Are you alright?" Sammy exclaimed, her voice cracked from tension. "No. Look, I have to make this fast.... Doti's going to look after you for a bit. They are keeping me at the hospital. Um, there was a bit of an incident."

"Oh, Dawson! Why did you have to say those things! I warned you it wouldn't go over well."

Sammy was very distressed now. She could hear the misery in his voice. "I don't know how long I'll be detained. I've really made a mess of things. I'm sorry Sammy. Look, I have to go."

"Dawson, I'll get you out of this. I'll set it right." Sammy paced around the handset. "That's a promise, and a cat always keeps her promises."

Dawson's voice sounded strained, as though he were trying to wrestle himself free of something. There were other voices too, firm voices that sounded quite unhappy.

"I have to go Sammy. Don't do anything foolish."

There was an audible click and then he was gone, leaving only a loud, repeating busy signal.

Now how long will I have to listen to that? Sammy thought irritably, as she sat and stared at the telephone.

CHAPTER FIFTEEN

BAD TO WORSE

Dawson had made quite a mess out of things indeed. The problem was, as he soon discovered, once some situations started to collapse there was no stopping them.

The situation Dawson had created without thinking had become a cascade effect. As with a house of cards, once a part of the foundation was removed, the whole thing came crumbling down around him.

What made it worse was trying harder to justify himself by further attempting to explain the truth of it all. It seemed the clearer he explained it – the crazier he sounded, even in his own ears.

Lying on the sterile sheets of the psychiatric ward in the hospital was giving Dawson plenty of time to reflect on everything. There was nothing else to do after all, other than look out the window. But he couldn't do that as he was cuffed down to the bed; an entirely unnecessary precaution. After all – it had not been his intention to strike Bartley Knight, it had just *happened*.

Dawson's stomach turned thinking about the events of the night before.

Ever notice how when we reflect on a situation, we are much better at seeing what it is we should or should not have done? Well, that is where poor Dawson was now, and he didn't much like how he had behaved.

The trouble was, after he was escorted off stage by a very angry Bartley Knight and his cohorts, it was Bartley, not Dawson who became violent.

He had roughed Dawson up a bit, grabbing him by the collar and shoving him against the wall. He had hollered in his face, threatened him, shoved him, and accused him of staging a publicity stunt on his show. Dawson had taken it all in stride, tried to keep his head, tried to explain; which of course only infuriated the talk show host even further.

Still, Dawson was not predisposed towards violence. He wasn't frightened so much by the unkind treatment he received, it wasn't the first time in his life someone bigger and stronger had tossed him about. He refused to engage in it - until Doti stepped in and tried to break them up.

When Knight shoved her off her feet was the moment Dawson lost his temper and he hit Bartley Knight square across the jaw.

In all honesty, he had not even realized his fist was clenched and he didn't realize he could be so fierce, but after all it was Doti.

And at that precise moment security tackled him to the ground and he made two trips from that point on; one to the police station and then onwards to the psychiatric ward of the hospital.

Another problem which arrived during his transition was that he was treated as though he were a lunatic. Rationally, he couldn't see any reason to have been antagonized the way he was throughout his ordeal. After all, Bartley had been the first to assault him; but once the talking cat came into it, every part of Dawson's good name was thrown out and all that was left was a man whom everyone began to refer to as the crackpot.

Now, laying in the bed and waiting for somebody to decide that he was neither a danger to himself or anyone else around him, Dawson began to feel a sensation that he knew must be depression.

Have you ever known something was true, yet not been able to prove it? Not a feeling or faith, but really known something was true because you had experienced it firsthand, yet because there was no other witness around to back up the story- nobody would believe you?

This was the underlying reality of his descent from a rather level mental state to being very unhappy. Dawson had never had anyone accuse him of being anything but honest to a fault. Yet now he was a liar or a mental defective. He was delusional, he was a cracker, and he was a nut job.

Nobody, not a one, including Doti, believed him.

The worst part of it was, he could hardly blame them – after all, not so very long ago he would have felt the same way. This was what arose from strict adherence to *The Natural Order of Things*. Not one person was open to investigating it further. Not one person said *'Hey, let's just say for the sake of argument he is, in fact, telling the truth.'*

It is a well-known and wildly accepted fact that cats *do not talk*. Not in a way people could ever understand. Animals do not think the way we do. They do not express themselves the way we do, they do not vocalize the way we do and they certainly do not collaborate with a human being to write a book.

But most importantly of all, they do not recollect the events of countless millennia and hold in their tiny minds the answers to some of the most difficult questions ever posed. It simply is not possible. Period.

Or is it?

Who has ever bothered to look into the matter anyways? The answer is very simple; *nobody*. Without the experience that Dawson had talking to his cat, without hearing the accounts firsthand that she had to share, there was no hope for humanity at large to accept his words.

Maybe, Dawson thought sadly, people just didn't want to try to accept that something so farfetched could be real. After all, if they accepted that, how much else would they have to change? And humans are notoriously opposed to change unless it creeps up on them; *very, very slowly.*

"Hello, Mr. Parks. How are you feeling this morning?" It was a new nurse, Betty by the name tag. The one he had last night had likely gone home already. Dawson didn't bother to look at her. He just stared at the ceiling.

"I'd be a great deal better if I wasn't strapped down."

"Yes, of course. Doctor Lamb has approved the removal of your restraints. However, if you decide to act out again, we shall have to put you back in them. Understand?" Nurse Betty talked very sweetly -almost too sweetly – as though she were humoring a child.

Dawson did not appreciate being condescended to, but he held his tongue. After all, he wanted to be set free. The nurse made quick work of releasing him and he sat up gratefully, rubbing his wrists.

"Thank you." Dawson stretched widely. Several joints popped in protest of having had to be in one position far too long.

"The doctor wishes to see you now. Follow me." With that, she turned and exited the room in full expectation that he would do as he was told. Dawson fell in behind her, uncertain as to what would come next; but anything was better than being locked up in that room.

Dr. Lamb's office was not as modern in appearance as the rest of the hospital. He had a grand old oak desk and several bookshelves shoved full of what appeared to be every book on psychology ever written. Dawson wondered if he had actually read them all, or if some were just there for show.

The good doctor himself was much older than Dawson, likely by nearly a quarter century. He was fit, tall and had that air about him that most prestigious intellectuals bore. The doctor sat in his overstuffed leather office chair flipping through a medical chart, on his desk was a copy of Dawson's book and a fat Russian Blue cat with luminous green eyes and a posh looking braided blue collar.

"Hello." Dawson said to the cat as he took a seat in the chair opposite the desk. The cat, of course, said nothing, closing his eyes and turning away.

"He doesn't talk, if that's what you are wondering." The doctor chuckled and closed the file folder. "Archimedes doesn't much care for strangers either, but once he gets to know you, he may warm up."

"Archimedes?" Dawson repeated back, a little sheepishly. The cat looked back at him and his ears turned back a bit.

"Yes. After the Greek mathematician." The doctor set the file folder down on his desk.

"I know who Archimedes was." Dawson crossed his arms over his chest and settled in for what was to come.

The doctor appraised him a moment before indicating the book. "I read your book last night. Very creative, a good start for a career in writing fiction."

"Thank you. But it is not my intention to become a writer." Dawson looked at the cat again, who blinked and then closed his eyes as though drowsing off.

"Oh? Well, that's too bad. You have a gift." The doctor had a look in his eye and a tilt to his tone that made Dawson think of a professional chess player.

"Not my gift." Dawson shrugged. "I only compiled the thing. But I think you already know that."

Dr. Lamb leaned forward onto the desk. "I have seen the video of last night's broadcast, yes. I have read the report. Seems you got quite violent after the show towards Mr. Knight. He has stated he will not be pressing charges, granted that you get therapy."

"Funny, he assaulted me. I only struck him due to his shoving my girlfriend when she tried to stop him." Dawson felt quite aggravated by the obviously one-sided report that was made.

"Did he now? I didn't see any of that from the witness statements." Dr. Lamb opened the file folder and began to rifle through. "Nothing. Sorry. According to the reports you hit him without provocation."

"What about my girlfriend Doti? Did she not make a statement?" Dawson arched a brow. It seemed unlikely Doti would have said nothing...

"I'm afraid not Dawson." The doctor sighed.

"Well, then it's my word against his." Dawson glowered.

"It would seem so, yes." Dr. Lamb closed the file again, then pulled out a little voice recorder from his desk. "So tell me about this cat of yours Dawson. I would rather like you to start from the beginning and work your way to where we are now. I want you to be honest, of course, and factual if you can."

"Sure. I will try." Dawson wasn't sure where the doctor was going with this, but given his circumstances, he saw no other recourse but to comply.

CHAPTER SIXTEEN

OUT OF THE BAG

It took only a little less than an hour, much to Dawson's surprise, to summarize the happenings of the past months. But he supposed time must be easier to condense in words than space.

Dr. Lamb listened patiently throughout, only interrupting occasionally to ask for clarity or further details on one thing or another. When they were finished, Dawson felt very fatigued, and yet lighter somehow, having shared it; even if there was no way the doctor would ever believe him.

"I see, I see." Dr. Lamb said as Dawson finished speaking. He turned off the voice recorder and set it back into his desk.

"Dawson, now you must understand that cats do not in fact talk."

"Not all of them, no." Dawson was sitting with his elbows on his knees, and his head in his hands. They had already been at this verbal jousting match for an hour and he was wearing out. "Only some can. Sort of the same way that only some people can speak other languages. Like Swahili."

Dr. Lamb sighed. "Dawson, what you experienced.......... it wasn't real. I want to run some tests, and in the meantime, I shall be giving you some medications. I promise you they will make you feel much better – make you see things a bit more clearly"

Dawson didn't look up. "What I experienced was real. The cat can talk. Go ask her."

He shot an exasperated look over at Archimedes, but he was – apparently- sound asleep.

"Dawson really." The psychiatrist smirked. "Cats cannot talk, not the way a human does. They simply do not have the physiological capacity to do so. It is a well-documented, scientific fact."

Dawson sighed deeply and looked up. "Well documented. Scientific. Those words used to mean something to me you know. Now I just see them as a means to guard against the truth."

"I always thought they were there rather to protect it." Dr. Lamb didn't flinch.

Dawson sat back in his seat. "What is it anyways, truth? Really? Do you know?"

"Why don't you tell me?" Dr. Lamb's voice was irritatingly well-practiced at that exact phrase. Dawson knew he was not really interested in listening, though, he was interested in analyzing; Dawson had an experience nobody else had known. It was real, he knew it was real. All he could think to do now was try to make a valid argument. He could try to convince the doctor that he was rational, reasonable.

"Here is a reality for you: Mercury. People used it to kill lice by rubbing it on their skin. They also put it in tonics and concoctions to cure various conditions. *Mercury* of all things. But it was a widely acceptable truth. Even scientifically accepted."

"That was a long time ago. Obviously, we have learned that it is a toxic substance since then." Dr. Lamb shrugged.

"Yes, but, at the time, it was truth. Just like at this time you hold dear to many so called truths that in a hundred years' time, people will be saying: I really can't believe they did that or believed in that."

Dawson speared his fingers through his hair. "Is it so hard to accept that something you believe, could be wrong? I had to; I had no real choice in the matter, and you know what? I'm glad for it. We all fumble about our lives just trying to adhere to the well-travelled path. We hold fast to the idea that change is good, and yet treat change with absolute disdain. It's madness."

"You have a disorder, Dawson. You hear your cat talking to you. Has anyone else ever spoken to the cat? Do you have any witnesses outside yourself? Can you verify your story?" Dr. Lamb leaned forward. He smiled, but not unkindly.

"No. She asked me not to tell anyone." Dawson lowered his head in defeat.

"Of course she would, wouldn't she?" The doctor took a deep breath. "You have had an episode. Perhaps brought on by stress, perhaps it is a condition. But either way, Dawson, you will have to make peace with this."

This was a battle he could not win. He remembered what Sammy had said about the darkness of human beings and what they did to things they did not understand. Even if he could bring the cat here, get her to talk to the good doctor, what then?

Would his dear little cat be whisked off to a laboratory to be studied? She might be treated like a lab rat, poked and prodded and subjected to experimentation. Sammy would be miserable.

He hadn't considered that while he had been fighting so hard to be believed. Dawson knew at once he had been selfish. Determined to clear his own name and for what? He needed to get home. He had made a grievous mistake and obviously trying to convince this other man that what happened had truly taken place was pointless. Without directly experiencing what he had, Dr. Lamb would refuse to take Dawson at his word. So, with a heavy heart, he decided to retract his claim.

He knew he had to lie; that a lie was the only truth that anyone would accept from him in this case. He let out a long, slow breath.

"I can't do this."

"Do what Dawson?" Dr. Lamb's brow furrowed.

"It was a publicity stunt. To sell my books. Nothing more. I was going to drag it out for a while, but, I just can't sit here feeding you line after line. I'm not that type of person." Dawson made himself meet the doctor's gaze.

"I see." Dr. Lamb sat forward. "Did someone put you up to this Dawson?"

"Yes. Just some poor advice." Dawson rubbed his temple. "Can I go home?"

"Well, not just like that. You certainly changed your story in a hurry. After your outburst at the studio, you are also expected to spend some time under psychiatric evaluation." Dr. Lamb looked at him with a hint of suspicion. "I'm going to keep you here for a few weeks, and run those tests. Just as a precaution Dawson. You will be required to take the prescribed medicines as well. Once again, precautions. If what you say is true, I imagine you should owe an apology to Mr. Knight."

"Of course." Dawson just wanted to go back to his room now. He was done.

"So then, you admit the cat cannot talk?" Dr. Lamb pressed a bit further. Dawson looked over at the doctor's own cat, who was not being very helpful at all. Must be one of those slower cats, he thought with disdain.

"Yes," Dawson stated solemnly. "Sammy Jack never spoke."

Meanwhile, back at his apartment, Doti had just let herself inside. The phone was off the hook, the TV was on, and Sammy Jack looked none too happy sitting in the window having had to listen to the racket all night. She stretched and yawned as Doti hung up the phone and turned the television off. In her hand was the morning paper which bore a headline on the front page that read in big bold letters:

THE CAT'S OUT OF THE BAG: AUTHOR CLAIMS CAT CAN TALK

Sammy hopped down from the window and jaunted over to Doti, who looked very upset. She bent down and pet Sammy. "You poor little thing. You're probably hungry."

Doti sniffled and walked into the kitchen. She set the paper down on the counter and opened the cupboard door to get out a tin of cat food. "Dawson's going to be away for a little while Sammy. But don't worry. I'll look after you."

The cat's mind was full of questions.

When would Dawson be home? How long would he be locked away? Was he all right? She knew none of those questions would be answered unless she took action. So she did.

"Doti, there's something you might need to know about me."

Doti turned very slowly and looked down at her. Her eyes were very wide. Sammy continued. "You see...... well... Dawson wanted to tell you the truth. I asked him not to."

"You....... you *talked.*" Doti's face was very white.

"I spoke... yes." This all felt very familiar to Sammy, and she wished to perhaps skip this process.

"Oh my god!" Doti shrieked and ran out of the kitchen rushing around with no particular direction in mind. "Oh, my god....... Oh! I must be imagining this!"

"Doti.... please stop." Sammy tried to keep pace with her.

Doti shrieked again and ran up onto the couch. As though Sammy Jack were a spider she needed to get away from.

"You talked again!"

"I spoke again, yes Doti. Do we really need to go through this whole experience?" Sammy shook her head and sighed. There was no dealing with humans.

Doti paused and stared at her. Her voice was squeaky and tremulous. "He said you could talk. I didn't believe him."

"Of course you didn't. Most people wouldn't." Sammy jumped up on the corner of the couch.

"But you are talking!" Doti's tone had a very unusual tenor to it. Her breath was coming in short quick gasps.

"Yes. You should really calm down...." Sammy stood as she saw Doti's balance waiver. She blinked a few times at the cat and then fell into an unconscious heap onto the couch cushions.

Sammy walked over and looked at her. At least she had decided to not lock herself up in the bathroom. The little cat sighed and shook her head. "I really need to learn to wait until after they feed me to talk."

CHAPTER SEVENTEEN

EMPIRICAL EVIDENCE

Much to Sammy Jacks' surprise, Doti adapted much more quickly to the notion that cats can indeed talk. After she woke up and had another little fit, Sammy finally managed to get her to calm down and be reasonable.

She had sat on the couch and listened very quietly to the cat tell the story of how Dawson and she wrote the book. After it was all said and done, Doti stared at her a moment, stood, and then walked into the kitchen to make some tea.

She even remembered to feed Sammy while she was in there, for which Sammy was very much appreciative. With her tea in hand, she sat back down on the couch and tried to get things straight in her head. "So Dawson is *not* crazy." She stated. "You can talk. Cats, at least some of them, do remember everything."

"Yes." Sammy confirmed with a nod.

Doti took a few deep, calming breaths. "We shall have to go get Dawson out of that hospital then."

"I was hoping you might suggest that." Sammy Jack gave her the best feline smile she could manage, which of course startled Doti enough to make her drop her tea.

The plan was simple enough. Go to the hospital, see Dr. Lamb, and spring Dawson from the looney bin. The application of that plan was less simple than its concept, however.

Doti had to go buy a cat carrier to bring Sammy along for the trip. When she returned, she called a taxi to take them to the hospital.

It was a media circus outside, as reporters waited to see if they might get a snippet of something to report about Dawson Parks.

Luckily, Doti's face was not well known to the media, but just in case, she had worn a scarf and shades. She felt very much like a woman in one of those spy films Dawson liked so much, although she was sure she had neither the stature nor glamor of those Hollywood actresses.

The hospital itself was a maze of corridors and wards and she was warned right away which places did not allow any pets and that she would be expected to keep the animal contained. When she did find where Dr. Lamb's office was, he was with another client. She and Sammy had to wait over an hour before he emerged.

"Doctor Lamb?" Doti called as he said goodbye to a client and handed a file folder to his receptionist.

"Hello. What can I do for you?" Dr. Lamb reached out a friendly hand and Doti took it.

"My name is Doti Thomas. I understand you are treating my boyfriend, Dawson Parks?" Doti felt incredibly nervous.

"Oh! Yes. How good to meet you. What can I do for you, Miss Thomas?" Dr. Lamb smiled warmly; he was not at all as intimidating as Doti was expecting him to be.

Then, she had never met a real psychiatrist and only had TV shows and books to reference what their personality traits might be.

"Well, I was hoping to perhaps have a word, please. It's about Dawson and the events last night. If you are not too busy."

Her stomach was full of knots while he pondered a moment and looked at his watch.

"Well, you are in luck. I have twenty minutes before I have to attend a board meeting. Please, come in." He held the door to his office open and invited her inside.

Doti went back for the carrier but Dr. Lamb stopped her. "Sorry, but the little kitty cat will need to wait outside. I have my own cat in here today and yours might cause a stir."

"Oh....... all right." Doti shot Sammy an apologetic look and walked into the office, leaving the carrier and its inhabitant in the empty waiting room.

The office itself proved to be exactly what she expected of a psychiatrist's office, even down to the big antique oak desk and overstuffed leather office chair. She supposed some stereotypes must be true.

"Lovely office." She commented with honest appreciation. As a big reader of books, she loved to see shelves full of interesting materials.

"Thank you. Please, have a seat, Miss Thomas." Dr. Lamb indicated a comfortable looking chair and took his own place behind his desk as Doti sat. "Now, what is it you came to discuss?"

Doti steeled her nerves and swallowed hard. The doctor's big gray cat was lazing on the corner of his desk and regarded Doti with casual interest. She decided it might be best to just get to the point. "Well, you see, I think there has been a misunderstanding. In regards to Dawson that is."

Doti fidgeted with her handbag. Dr. Lamb leaned back in his chair. "Oh? And what is that?"

"Dawson.... he's not crazy." Doti forced an amicable smile.

"Nobody likes to use that kind of term around here, Miss Thomas. He has a disorder." Dr. Lamb crossed his arms.

"Although I am not able to discuss further than that; doctor - patient confidentiality, you understand?"

"Yes. But you must understand, and believe me when I tell you; you are mistaken." Doti pressed gently.

Dr. Lamb sighed. "Oh, the publicity stunt? I see. It was your idea."

"What? No! What are you talking about?" Doti cleared her throat. "No, I meant about the cat. His cat, Sammy Jack and her talking to him."

"Good grief!" He chuckled. "You don't honestly believe that the cat was actually talking to him."

"Yes. Because she was – is – able to talk. In fact, many cats can. They just don't because it might cause problems for them." Doti felt her face flush.

Dr. Lamb's face went icy and forebodingly calm. "Cat's do not talk, Miss Thomas."

Doti felt her pulse quicken. "Look, I brought the cat so she could tell you herself. If you just let me go get her…."

"No. That is unnecessary." Dr. Lamb laced his fingers on top of his desktop. "Is this some kind of joke Miss Thomas?"

"No. Not at all, if you would just let me go get her, she doesn't need to come out." Doti started to stammer.

For a man that had been so warm and welcoming moments ago, he was suddenly very intimidating. Doti felt tears welling up in her eyes. Why not just let her bring Sammy in? What could it hurt? She cast a desperate glance over at the gray cat that was now paying rapt attention to the dialogue.

"I am a busy man Miss Thomas. I have taken a moment out of concern for your man to listen to what you had to say, but this is a blatant waste of my time. And if you truly believe in the nonsense you are talking, well, perhaps you should be seeking help as well." Dr. Lamb's voice clipped with irritation.

"Please! I'm telling you, Dawson isn't crazy! Sammy Jack CAN talk! Just listen …." Doti was pleading now. All she wanted him to do was give her a chance to prove it.

"Have you completely lost your mind miss? Is this an epidemic of insanity? CATS SIMPLY DO NOT SPEAK." Doctor Lamb glared contemptuously at poor Doti whose face was now riddled with hot tears.

116

The gray cat rose to a seated position and yawned. He looked from Doti to Dr. Lamb and sighed. "Well actually, we do."

At first the doctor simply blinked at Doti. After all, she had said something, but her lips hadn't moved at all and she suddenly sounded very masculine as well.

"Pardon me?"

"I said: Actually we do."

Again her lips didn't move, and he also noticed that the voice was coming more from the side of his desk, not from in front of him. The doctor turned towards his own cat and his jaw dropped open. "A-Archimedes?"

"And on that note, I might add that *Samuel* was actually the name my previous owner gave me before you took me on. I must say, I have always wanted to tell you how much I *despise* the name, *Archimedes.*"

Doti chuckled in spite of herself and Archimedes-aka Samuel- winked at her.

"O-oh dear." It was precisely at that moment the doctor fell out of his chair.

"Go get your friend, dear." Archimedes directed Doti softly. "Sammy Jack and I have a great deal to discuss with the good doctor."

Doti smiled, tears streaming down her cheeks. "Thank you......... oh thank you so much...."

EMPIRICAL EVIDENCE

CHAPTER EIGHTEEN

THE PROMISE OF A CAT

The locked door to Dawson's room opened, but he didn't bother looking up. The medication they had given him to cure him of his 'condition' had him in a stupor; that and the knowledge that for the rest of his days he would either be known as that crazy cat guy or that slimy novelist.

He would be the writer who pulled that terrible publicity stunt just to increase his book sales. Between those two options, Dawson thought that crazy might be better than underhanded.

"Mr. Parks?" It was Dr. Lamb's voice, but Dawson didn't bother to acknowledge. He had nothing further to say to the psychiatrist. After all, anything he said would and could be used against him, so in that case, what was the point? Silence was indeed golden.

"Dawson?" Dr. Lamb sat on the edge of his bed; Dawson sat up and pulled his knees to his chest as he leaned back against the wall. He glanced at the doctor, who looked a bit shaken.

"Look, I know you may not wish to speak with me just now. But it seems I might owe you an apology." Dr. Lamb indeed looked quite shaken.

"What do you mean? Why?" Dawson looked at him intently. What was the game here? What did he want?

"Well, let's just say you have very convincing and very dedicated friends." Dr. Lamb looked back towards the door and made a motion with his hand beckoning somebody to enter. Doti stepped into the room followed by Sammy Jack.

"She told me, Dawson. She told me everything and she told him too." Doti's eyes were red and wet. Dawson looked down at the little ginger cat and his own eyes began to water.

"I made you a promise Dawson. That I would set things right. A cat always keeps her promises, you know." She took a tentative step towards him then stopped. "I'm so sorry Dawson. I'm so very sorry to have caused all of this trouble."

"It's all right Sammy. It was my own doing. I'm simply no good at lying." Dawson felt hot tears rolling down his cheeks now. "I'm the one who's sorry - for telling your secret."

Sammy Jack plodded up to the bed and crawled onto his legs. She bumped her head against his chin affectionately. "Well, now that it's all sorted, why don't we go home? I'm terribly hungry and you know you always feel better when you serve me my dinner."

At that, all of them started laughing - except for Sammy Jack, who looked very perplexed. "You know; I don't see how that's funny. I thought all humans felt better when they fed their pets. You seem to be very eager to do it."

"Of course we are Sammy." Dawson laughed, petting her head. "Of course."

Outside the media circus was in full swing. Dr. Lamb placed a reassuring hand on Dawson's shoulder as he walked towards the stairs with Sammy Jack in his arms. Doti was beside him and rubbed his back.

Cameras flashed and people crowded. The whole scene made him feel sick to his stomach and disjointed. He was about to lie to the whole world because the world would not accept his word and somehow that hurt worse than anything he had felt in his entire life.

He, Dr. Lamb and Doti had decided that despite the negative repercussions that would follow, it was best to claim the whole incident on *Nights with Knight Live* as a publicity stunt.

Somehow, Dr. Lamb had been able to negotiate with Knight's producer to make him corroborate the story, as Doti had explained in detail that Bartley Knight had indeed assaulted Dawson first. That Dawson had only acted in her defense.

Since Dawson had no interest in pursuing a career as an author, he didn't see the harm in ruining his notoriety in that field. The problem was that he would have to lie, and Dawson was terrible at lying.

In his arms, Sammy Jack rested placidly, taking in the excitement rather too calmly. Doti gave Dawson a reassuring smile as he approached the fray. They were all talking at him at once, questions upon questions, upon questions all falling against themselves until one could hardly understand a word.

"Dawson! Can you tell us what happened?" One reporter managed to stand out from the crowd.

He paused. "I…. Well you see, I was under a great deal of stress."

The reporters were not waiting for him to finish his sentence. More questions poured out. Was this really a publicity stunt? Is it true you have had issues with drug addiction? Do you really believe your cat talks to you? Do you often hear voices? Can you speak to dogs as well?

Dawson was trembling. It was too much. Even though he tried to steel himself, their onslaught was relentless. Sammy Jack shifted in his grasp as he tried again. "I…….. It was all…. it was just……."

Sammy looked up at Dawson then said: "Let me go."

"What? No…. Sammy." Dawson mumbled, trying not to look at her.

"It's okay Dawson. Let me go now."

Dawson's face was ruddy and his eyes were red from the strain he was under. Carefully, he set his little cat down and the crowd backed up a bit, calming slightly if only from perplexity.

With her plume of a tail held very high, Sammy approached the reporters. She stood and blinked at the crowd for a moment before clearing her voice.

"Dawson Parks is not crazy."

The little cat raised her voice and the crowd went dead silent as all eyes turned towards her.

"I can speak."

Sammy Jack took another tentative step forward. "A great many of us can. You simply don't understand, so you dismiss us. But here I am and I will speak with all of you now."

Dawson felt his trembling ease away as he stared at the suddenly silent mob. Doti slipped her hand into his as they let the crowd take in the information.

After all, human beings are notoriously slow at absorbing new ideas. Especially ideas like that of a cat talking back in a way they could understand.

EPILOGUE

Far out in the countryside, on a winding country road, over a bridge, and across a perfectly serene babbling brook is where this story comes to a close, and where an entirely different sort begins.

After Sammy Jack's dramatic revelation to the masses of indeed being capable of speech, and clearing once and for all poor Dawson's name, the world of both cat and man changed.

There were many busy days spent being whisked around one place to the next, many talk shows, many interviews, and much more questions than either Dawson or Sammy could ever wish to answer again over the remainder of their lifetime.

They even made a few re-appearances on Nights with Knight, although Bartley Knight was much more cordial with Dawson that time around. Especially since the ratings, those nights were through the roof.

They traveled overseas and posed for photo shoots, booking signings and were even asked to host their own TV show; Dawson wasted no time refusing that offer.

It took people quite a long stretch to finally accept that animals may indeed be able to talk in a way people could understand and Sammy Jack unwittingly became their ambassador.

She did indeed consider that to be quite the accomplishment.

The world began to change. It was the same sort of paradigm shift for most human beings that Dawson had experienced.

Unfortunately, those who were unwilling to accept this new change in the *Natural Order of Things* caused quite a lot of trouble for those that did for a while.

However, the notion that: Just because you think something is real doesn't make it real at all, had become a slogan, a banner that rose to help facilitate the change.

You see, most of what was bad in the world, most of the arguing and the conflict, was mostly due to the solidarity of knowing that what you believe in is absolutely true.

It had caused a great deal of trouble for the human race for a much longer time than it ever should have, and that is of course why Sammy Jack asked Dawson to write the book, to begin with.

As the message spread, one could see it on banners and buses, buildings, classrooms and even on T-shirts. People also began to follow a second rule: You must accept that everything you know, everything you have ever known, and everything you will ever know should always remain in question.

With the combination of those two mentalities in place, there was a resurgence in the curiosity of humankind; that same curiosity that allowed us to do and create many marvelous things, and of course, a better state of living for our cats.

All through this, Sammy Jack and her friend Dawson Parks drifted ever so slowly out of the limelight until once again, they were able to enjoy a day without an interview or a phone call.

It was around that time that Dawson got down on one knee and proposed to his beloved Doti; not with a ring, but with a deed. The deed was to a little old farmhouse in the center of a field in the countryside. It was surrounded by wildflowers and had a beautiful patch of lavender growing right in the front garden.

On that farm, Dawson and Doti retired from their old lives to start anew and there they started a sanctuary not just for cats, but for any animal that needed to find someplace safe to be. Although most did not speak like a cat, they were always understood, and as Sammy Jack would often say:

Not every creature can speak like a cat, but if one listens and understands them, they are just fine with that.

A MESSAGE FROM JINXI BLUE

If you took the time to read this novella I would love to hear
back from you.
You can reach me by email at:
jennyjinxiblue@gmail.com

I try to respond to every email as quickly as time allows.
Be patient and I will do my very best to respond personally to
your correspondence in a timely fashion.

ABOUT THE AUTHOR

Originally from the west coast of British Columbia, Jenny "Jinxi Blue" Laberge now lives on the opposite end of the map in Moncton, New Brunswick, Canada along with her beloved family and her little ginger cat named Pippin.

She has been writing stories since she could speak but has only just started her journey as an author.

Made in the USA
San Bernardino, CA
14 October 2017